Surviving
The
Game

Kat Green

1

There was a thunderous noise as the door to the club restaurant swung open hitting the wall. The team players were hungry after that morning's training session. Loud laughter turned into hooting over a joke one of the boys had made. Zara could not help but stare. A set of eyes caught hers for a split second and she immediately knew who it was.

"I'm starving," the owner of the eyes yelled rubbing his hands together. It was Zara's first week as a kitchen assistant for Valcoast United Football club. After a few days of training for the needs of the team this would be the first time she'd fully meet the first team squad. Jenny, her new boss, glided around the kitchen confident and fiercely protective of 'her boys'. Almost like a proud mother. Thankfully, she greeted the team first giving Zara a moment to compose herself.

"Do you ever stop eating?'' Jenny questioned. The player smiled. "I'm an elite athlete. Food is my fuel.'' That player was the team's goalkeeper, Ben Virgo. His well-built frame dwarfed the man standing beside him.

Zara knew all the faces as they approached the counter. Billy Fox, one of the team's strikers, looked up at the goalkeeper.

"He hasn't been stopping the goals from hitting the back of his net, though.'' Billy laughed at his own joke while looking around for support from his fellow players. They shook their heads instead. Ben looked down with a hint of irritation. The saying '*if looks could kill*' sprang to Zara's mind.

"I'll snap you in half, Foxy.'' Ben's tone stopped the cocky striker from making any further comments.

Keith, a part-time cook for the club was laughing to himself, shaking his head. He was a man of few words, but very skilled in the kitchen.

"Here we go, the banter begins," he mumbled while working over the large chrome pot.

Zara felt star-struck but forced herself to be professional. She focused on filling the baskets with breads, rolls, and fruit before checking all the various drinks machines around the restaurant. Every match was a sell-out, and it was deafening when it was full.

Zara hadn't met the Valcoast United players until now, and it was a surreal moment for her. She'd seen them on television, shouted at them from her sofa, and cheered for them from the stands with her family. Now she was part of the small but important catering team an opportunity she had taken without hesitation. She replaced an employee who had sold stories to the press involving club matters that had no right to be out in public. Several of these articles had caused distress to players' families, especially the ones that were bold lies. When Zara was hired, it was made clear to her that trust was important.

''Don't stare,'' her boss whispered. ''I know it seems like a dream, but they're just human beings.'' Zara nodded and smiled as the team's goalkeeper approached first.

''You're new,'' he smiled turning to Jenny. ''Jen, good to see they've finally gotten you support.''

''Yes, it was about damn time! Ben, I would like you to meet Zara,'' Ben nodded and flashed another warm grin in Zara's direction.

3

"Welcome to Valcoast United." Zara returned the smile as Hayden Palmer, the team captain and Left midfielder, walked up to the counter. Zara's nerves had hit, and she was afraid to say anything else. She didn't want to embarrass herself.

"All right Virgo…remember you're married," he grinned patting his teammate on the shoulder.

Hayden was famous for speaking his mind and had a reputation for being hardcore. He seemed scared of nothing, and he didn't play pretty football. He played hard and fierce. If blood gushed down his face, he'd carry on with a smile.

"I'm just being friendly," returning his gaze to Zara. "I swear that's all."

Hayden winked at her from behind Ben. A smirk on his face. Ben was taller and broader in the flesh while Hayden seemed shorter, but his presence oozed authority and experience. His career was nearing the end. Thirty-four in football was considered old. He'd done it all and directed the team like a drill sergeant. Winning was all he cared about. He hated show-offs, and if you were selfish on the pitch, he'd remind you who was the captain. He would be a fantastic manager once his playing career ended.

Loud laughter from the back of the room made her look over. Players bantered with each other before noticing the unfamiliar face. Hayden called for their attention. 'Lads, this is Zara. Be nice.''

Ben looked offended.

''I think that's what I was doing while you were telling me to remember I'm married,'' he scowled at his captain. ''I fucking know I'm married. I was there when we both said, 'I Do'!'' Cackles echoed around the room.

''Oh...calm down, Virgo. Did he hit a nerve?'' Billy Fox braved the conversation. He was one of the younger players. Nineteen, going on dead if his comments continued. Ben wasted no time in his comeback.

''At least he can hit something. How 'bout you shut your mouth and find the back of the fucking net?'' Ben glanced between Billy and Zara, a roguish smile on his face. "Oh, were you showing off for Zara?'' he taunted. Billy concealed his embarrassment. He hated when Ben was right.

"When Mads gets in here, I bet a week's wages you won't stand a chance,'' he pointed at the youngster.

Hayden cocked his head towards the conversation, then back at Zara, noticing the awkward look on her face.

"Have a bit of respect, lads. She's not a doll in a window shop.''

Billy looked guilty, ''Sorry, it's just jokes.'' His features softened even though he'd been told off and belittled in front of her. Although to be fair, he had started it. Zara felt a little sorry for him until he opened his mouth again.

"Anyway, who says Mads would be interested in a kitchen girl.''

The looks on the rest of the team's faces were priceless! Shakes of heads, calls of 'for fuck's sake Billy', 'shut the fuck up', or similar came at him from every table.

Hayden got up from his chair and walked over to Zara, "Take no notice, he's young and stupid and means no harm.'' His rugged features seemed concerned. "He doesn't mean to be a disrespectful arse. He'll eventually learn...''

"It's okay. I know. Who's' Mads, anyway?''

Hayden smiled. ''Oh, that'll be Jake.'' Before Zara could respond, the tense situation eased as Billy threw a roll at the head of the goalkeeper. Ben's quick reflexes ensured he caught it and returned it, hitting Billy square between the eyes, causing more hysterics and the banter continued. Zara couldn't help but join in the laughter.

''I love this place,'' Jenny giggled beside Zara. ''You alright? They haven't upset you?''

"No, I'm made of harder stuff than a few jokes." In fact, Zara was already falling in love with her new job. Jenny nodded and continued cutting bread. ''That's good.''

Zara scanned the room, taking in the faces of the Valcoast United players, whose culinary needs were now in her hands. The door opened, one more player entered the room. Jake Maddox, star striker and Valcoast's golden boy. This had to be Mads. He held himself like he knew he was a star. They paid him two hundred and fifty thousand pounds a week. The highest-paid player on the team.

''Here comes trouble,'' Jenny whispered. ''Amazing player, and hot, as you've noticed.'' Zara had noticed, and he was better in the flesh. Tall, robust, there was no doubt he was a powerful force on the pitch. Zara's nan would describe him as a strapping young man. "Big reputation, on and off the pitch, but he's harmless, though. Not as bad as the press makes out,'' Jenny continued.

Jake approached the counter, leaning on it.

''Hello Jake,'' Jenny greeted him with a smile. ''Keeping out of trouble?''

Jake placed his hand to his chest in mock horror, "I am offended you even need to ask. I am an angel.''

His sea-blue eyes were piercing, the wavy, medium-long blonde hair gave him an Indie band look, and he knew he could charm the birds from the trees. Zara knew she was staring but struggled to look away. He didn't seem to notice or care.

''I just saw a pig fly past the window,'' Jenny joked. She introduced Zara to him. He'd already noted the fresh face. There was a silence before he spoke.

''Nice to meet you, Zara,'' Jake said before taking his food and sitting with the goalkeeper and Billy Fox, Jake's strike partner, which gave her no time to respond. It was a good thing she had momentarily lost the ability to speak.

"What did I fucking say, Foxy?'' Ben cackled as Jake took a seat. Billy threw Ben a look that said, '*Shut up*!'

It wasn't long before her nerves settled, and she felt completely at ease. The atmosphere was friendly, and most players took the time to welcome her. Even though Zara was relaxing, she remembered the strict policy Jenny had mentioned during her interview…

It might be the club restaurant, but it's a very important job. You meet the needs of the players, management, and anyone else who comes in. Question nothing. It's not our business, no matter how odd the request might seem. And never talk about anything you see or hear in this club. We are important. We mess up in here and they don't get what they need. On the pitch, it could make all the difference.

''I see you morons are acting up because there is a fresh face. Virgo, you're married, remember? Jenna would bury you,'' Jake Maddox bantered.

He tilted his head in Zara's direction. He caught her eye for a few seconds before Billy flicked him in the face for no other reason but to annoy or humiliate. Jake glared at him before shoving food in his mouth with a shake of his head. Hysterical laughter continued to fill the room.

Ben held his arms in the air.

''What is this… take the piss out of Virgo day? I was being nice, you fucking pricks.''

He snuck a glance to Zara, ''But it is true, Jenna would kill me.'' He winked and returned to his food.

Giggling, Jenny assured her Ben wasn't flirting.

''Ben and Jenna are a great couple. Genuine love…it's very sweet. They like to make him out as a playboy, to cover their misadventures. A past he's well and truly put behind him.''

Moving on, Jenny pointed to a few meals prepared for specific players. There had been intense training on special requirements. Now it was time to prove she could do this. She picked up a tray prepared for Alvaro Garrido, the Spanish Right Back, who sat alone at a table. A book in his hand, he seemed he was in his own world…an air of arrogance surrounding him.

''You need to take it to him. He doesn't come to us,'' Jenny said. Zara looked at her.

''Question nothing,'' Jenny reminded her. She could feel Jenny's eyes watch her as she crossed the room. Alvaro didn't look up as she placed the tray on the table. Awkward, she thought. His hand reached for the tray. As Zara turned, Jenny was glaring. She'd just failed at something. She flicked her head back to the tray shaking her head No!

There was dairy on the tray, and Alvaro was allergic to dairy. Zara grabbed the tray pulling it away. Alvaro looked up and he smiled.

''Bravo!'' he said, his accent thick. The cold aura vanished. He smiled and then laughed loudly.

''Thank god, Zara, I was about to have a heart attack,'' Jenny remarked grabbing the tray from me.

Suddenly, the room roared with laughter. ''That was a test?'' Zara cried, looking around in confusion. Jenny nodded.

'You bastards! That's not funny!'' She yelled.

Jenny smiled and waved her back, ''Ahh, but you won't do it again.''

It took a long time for her heart to stop hammering in her chest. ''Why would you risk that?''

''Did you nearly kill my right back?'' a stern Yorkshire accent boomed from behind Zara. She knew that voice. Ted Huxley, the manager. Zara spun to face him. He towered over her, kitted out in a club tracksuit that clung to his middle-aged spread. His hair greying at the sides of his stern face.

''I'm so sorry,'' her words breaking on their way out. ''I really am.''

Ted continued to glare at her. He was terrifying. The room was silent, nobody made a sound. All eyes were on her. It was mortifying. The ticking of a clock was all she could hear as the seconds ticked by. Finally, Ted straightened and smiled.

''You didn't kill him, so no harm done. I see they've wasted no time in pranking you. Stay alert Zara, this lot is feral,'' he held out his hand, and she shook it. ''Nice to meet you. By the way, he wouldn't have eaten it. It was perfectly safe. Now you are part of this unhinged family.''

The atmosphere eased and Alvaro nodded. "Es muy cierto,'' he said, then returned to his book. Zara didn't speak Spanish and her face made that clear. Ted rescued her, ''He said it's very true.''

The moment was interrupted with Jenny yelling as she wrestled with the coffee machine.

"This sodding thing keeps playing up.'' After a few minutes of shouting explicits, she had it working again. Taking a deep breath, her attention turned to the manager.

''Ted, you didn't come in for breakfast this morning. Now sit and I'll bring something over,'' Jenny scolded him. He rolled his eyes.

''I'm a grown man, Jen.'' She waved a hand to cut him off, ''I don't care. You need to eat, so sit down.''

A few minutes later, she placed a large coffee and a stack of toast in front of the distracted man. He acted irritated by her but appreciated her more than he would admit. Ted looked stressed and tired, and Zara wondered what went on in his mind. His team was doing terrible this season, and usually, they sat at least top ten of the premier league. They were barely above the relegation zone in seventeenth place. Thirty-nine points was all they had picked up. That had all been at the start of the season. It was shocking for them. If Jake Maddox hadn't played so badly over the past few weeks, things would look different. Normally, he was a goal machine and scored in most games. It was rare to see him not score. For some reason, that had changed. It had been weeks since he'd found the back of the net. It was proof to the world just how much the club relied on him. Cardiff, Fulham, and Huddersfield all sat beneath them and a few wins for any of those teams would drop Valcoast United further down the list. It was getting closer to the Championship, and panic was setting in. The loud chat from the various tables masked the worries that simmered underneath.

The rest of the day passed quickly, and Zara was amazed at how many people she had met. Any fear she'd had before starting had gone. After a busy day of players, management, and important visitors to the club needing food and drinks, it was time to clean down and ready for the next day.

''Well done for today,'' praised Jenny as they locked up. ''I hope those idiots didn't scare you off.''

''Thanks! No, they didn't. I loved it.'' It was true, despite the prank, she had loved every second.

''I'm so sorry about Alvaro. It was cruel and I'm sorry. At least you didn't kill a sixty-five million pound Spanish right back. I mean, it wouldn't just be this club's problem. You'd have pissed off Spain too,'' Jenny roared with laughter. ''Those lads do much worse to each other. They are like schoolboys sometimes, with their pranks. It's rubbed off on me.''

"I think I might stick it out. Maybe I'll try taking out Jake tomorrow. How much is he worth?" Zara joked.

"Seventy-Six, I think."

"Quid? That's not worth my time."

"You'll do just fine here," Jenny laughed. Keep a sense of humour. You'll need it. By the way, could you start earlier tomorrow? It's a big game and it would be a massive help. Tina will be in tomorrow and I know you'll get on great with her, but there is so much to do. Can you be there by seven?" Jenny asked, hopefully.

"Sure," Zara agreed.

"Well, I'm off to deal with my lot at home," Jenny said as she walked with her to the staff carpark.

"Four teenage boys!" she said with a look of terror. "Love them, though." She waved as she got in her car.

Keith waved as he passed her, driving out of the carpark. He wasn't rude, just a little shy, Jenny had said. A skilled cook which was all that mattered. She waved and gave him a nod before getting in her car. The feeling of being part of something so deep-rooted into the city of Valcoast was exciting. Football was important here, and the history of the club started back in 1903.

As Zara drove slowly around the carpark heading for the exit, she spotted Jake Maddox beside his car, a Black Maserati. He stood talking to a man she'd not seen around the club. Something wasn't right. The conversation looked hushed but heated. The stranger leaned into Jake's ear, and whatever he said enraged the Striker. A scarf covered the face, and a black baseball cap obscured the rest. His identity was hard to make out. Jake pushed the guy away, and she only caught a split second of a shout, ''No, fuck off!''

Zara stopped her car and wound down her window, ''Jake, are you OK?''

Both men acted suspiciously. The stranger stepped back from Jake and pointed at her, ''who's this? New girlfriend?''

''No. She works here.'' Jake glowered at the stranger, then at Zara, ''I'm fine. Go home.''

It wasn't a request but a command. Reluctantly Zara did as he asked. As she pulled away, she took another look back. There was another angry exchange before both men parted ways. An unease settled over her, but it was none of her business, and getting involved wasn't her responsibility. Her phone ringing interrupted her thoughts. It was Dad calling wanting to hear how her first proper day had gone.

''Did you meet the whole team?'' He was like a child, excited to hear.

''Yes, I did.''

''What are they like? Did you meet Jake Maddox?''

''They all seemed lovely, and yes, I met Jake.'' He was her dad's favourite player. She left out the odd carpark incident.

''Cracking. You can give me all the club gossip now,'' he chuckled. ''I'm glad it's going well.'' After chatting a few more minutes, Zara said goodbye.

That was his day made, and Zara was sure he would brag to all his mates down at the pub later that night. She would have to remember to filter what she said to her dad. He was not good at being discreet.

As she drove home, she noticed a car behind her a little too close. Zara was certain the driver was the same man from the carpark. She kept calm as he could've been taking the same street, and eventually, he did turn a different way. She hadn't realised she had been holding her breath and laughed at herself for panicking. Her block of flats came into view and she looked forward to getting home and relaxing, but her best friend had other ideas.

"I want to hear all about your day! Drinks?"
Rachel was hard to turn down, "Come on,
please?"

"Fine, but I have to be in at work at seven, so two
drinks tops," Zara said firmly.

"Ok." Rachel giggled, "I'll see you at Vibe bar in
an hour." The chilled evening Zara had planned
wasn't happening. She raced up to her flat to get
ready.

2

The bar was busy when Zara arrived, and the Friday night drinkers were already in full swing. Vibe bar was a popular place often frequented by the players, although, it was highly doubtful they would be in tonight. She suspected Rachel had chosen it for that reason.

''Zara!'' Rachel shouted from a table in the corner. ''I've got cocktails,'' holding up her favourite drink, Purple Rain. It was a good start and she could never turn down a cocktail.

''How was today?'' Rachel didn't even try to hide her excitement. ''Tell me everything!''

''Can I at least take a sip of my drink first?''

''Fine.'' Rachel said with mock annoyance. Only waiting a short amount of time, she continued, ''how was your first week? Are you settled in…are they nice to you?''

Zara nodded, "it's been brilliant. Everyone seems so nice.''

She talked about her week. Rachel listened intently, and the two-drink rule quickly went out the window. It wasn't long before they were dancing on the dance floor. She had to admit it had been nice to catch up with Rachel. They didn't get to do it often with her friend working shifts as a care assistant at an old people's home. Plus, Zara had been getting her life back on track after her recent breakup, so she hadn't been very sociable.

''Now, you're single, you can upgrade and become a WAG,'' Rachel shouted over the music. She liked using the term for Wives and Girlfriends of the footballers.

''I'm good, thanks. After two years of that prick, I'll stay single,'' she shouted back. Rachel cheered at the mention of the EX.

The girls made their way back to the small table and collapsed, sweat running down their faces.

''I'm glad you're free from that piece of shit. I'm just saying you can have a bit of fun,'' Rachel winked.

''Maybe.'' Zara giggled.

It hadn't been a relationship, more like being caged and controlled. She didn't dwell on it; she was free. It was time to move on.

A few songs later Zara checked the time, ''I need to go soon.'' It was just after midnight. ''Seriously, one more dance and, I'm gone.'' Rachel accepted defeat and downed her drink. Zara booked an Uber, and they danced their way to the door.

''I didn't think they allowed players to drink before a game?'' Rachel asked, looking over Zara's head before getting out the door.

''They don't…''

''It looks as if Jake Maddox didn't get the memo, and he looks in a right state,'' Rachel nodded towards the bar.

Zara turned and sure enough, there was Jake, leaned up against the bar, a glass in his hand. Someone said something in his ear, and he ignored them. They persisted, and he reacted, his forehead almost touching the other guy's, his shoulders squaring up. ''It looks like it's about to kick off,'' Rachel warned.

''I have to get him out of here,'' Zara turned and yelled towards him.

''Jake!'' She shouted, ''Stop!'' He turned, trying to focus as it took him a few seconds to recognise her. He was drunk, and he stumbled backward.

''You know him?'' The bartender called to her, holding him up. Zara nodded…it was almost the truth. ''You need to sort him out. Go out the back.''

''I'm fine. You ain't my boss,'' he stumbled again, "stay out of my business.'' The bartender looked concerned and allowed Zara to guide him through the back and out through a side door. "I want another drink'' Jake demanded. They ignored his requests.

''Get him home, it won't be long before the press is all over this.'' The bartender gave full control to Zara and closed the door.

''I'll get the Uber and bring it 'round the back,'' Rachel offered and ran towards the front of the building in search of the driver.

''I don't need your help!'' Jake snapped. Zara ignored him, planting her feet firmly to adjust to his weight.

''What are you doing? You have Tottenham tomorrow!'' Zara scolded. Jake shrugged, pulling away from her grip.

''It's none of your business,'' he tried to walk away as the Uber pulled around the corner.

''Get in,'' Rachel shouted, ''there is press outside the front.'' The mention of press sobered Jake enough to take notice and he jumped in. Zara followed giving her address, and the car sped off. All she wanted was to get them out of the town centre. They could figure out their next step later. Jake put his head in his hands.

The reality was setting in, and he knew he'd royally screwed up. ''Oh shit.''

''Have you lost your mind?!'' Zara shouted. "You don't have many games left and you're sitting above relegation, with Spurs tomorrow,'' the fan in her exploded to the surface. ''People are relying on you tomorrow, and you're out getting smashed. You selfish prick!'' Jake looked insulted, but Zara didn't care. Rachel sat in the middle, her face showing pride at her best friend shouting at a highly paid, very famous footballer.

''Jake, this is my best friend Zara, a massive Valcoast United fan, and now, your only hope out of this mess,'' Rachel's laugh was borderline evil.

''Yeah, we've met for the third time today. She ain't my boss,'' he snapped.

''No, but if you want my help, don't push me!'' he groaned and he knew Zara was right. ''So, we go to mine and we get you sober. That's the first thing. Because hungover or not, you will play like a machine tomorrow as long as the club doesn't get wind of this and Ted bench's you!''

Fifteen minutes later, back at her flat, they forced Jake to drink plenty of water. Zara gave up her bed, and she set up the sofa.

''I can't take your bed!'' Jake protested.

''Look, I'm not the one playing in an important game tomorrow, and after tonight, if you don't score a hat-trick, god help you!'' Zara was so angry she couldn't help her angry taunts. ''What possessed you?!''

''It's not your problem,'' He snapped. ''Why are you getting involved? Who the fuck do you think you are?'' he was on the defensive, knowing full well he'd brought it all on himself. Zara picked up her phone, holding it up.

''OK, I'll call Ted, and I'll let him deal...''

''No! Don't do that!'' Jake cut her off. Holding his hands up in surrender, he sighed. ''Fine, I'll behave. What's your plan, Gaffer?'' The atmosphere eased, and he listened to her plan. He would stay, get some rest, and she'd drive him home on her way to work. He could get himself organised and get to the club on time. After more water and getting Rachel a cab home, they finally went to sleep. Although having Jake Maddox sleeping in your bed was not a usual Friday night.

Her alarm woke her at five-thirty, and she awkwardly opened the door to her room. Jake was sound asleep and a part of her wanted to let him stay that way. He looked younger, peaceful, but she had to wake him. Taking a few more seconds to soak in the reality that Jake Maddox was in her bed, she remembered where he needed to be. She pulled herself together, and placed her hand on his shoulder, shaking him half heartily at first. He didn't move. Several more attempts failed. It was like waking the dead. Leaning over him, her mouth near his ear, she yelled, "'Jake!''

His eyes opened, and he jolted upwards. "What the… where the fuck am I?" he rubbed his eyes. ''What happened?'' He looked at Zara utterly confused.

After a strong coffee, he remembered his previous night's actions.

''I'm sorry about last night,'' he said sheepishly. Embarrassment was etched all over his face. ''You won't tell anyone, will you?''

"I won't say anything, but people that saw you in the bar might.'' He sighed and put his head on the coffee table.

"I feel like shite,'' his hand went up. "I know! Before you say it…it's my own fault.''

Zara left him to wallow in self-pity, while she went to get ready for work. They left a few minutes later than planned, arriving at Jake's around six-thirty. He didn't get out straight away. He lingered a moment before speaking.

"Thank you for what you did for me. I'm sorry if I was a dick. You promise you and your friend won't tell anyone?"

Zara assured him they wouldn't say a word.

"Get yourself sorted, and I'll see you later. I want a hat-trick! Now, Go!" a slight smile spreading over Zara's face. He waved as she drove away.

Once she'd calmed down, she sent a quick text to Rachel telling her to keep their night to herself. She responded quickly assuring her she'd say nothing.

Driving the rest of the way to work, she thought about Jake's odd behaviour. As far as she knew, Jake didn't do things like that. Why now? Unless he trusted her to know, she would have to put last night down to experience. Her focus was on work, and with two minutes to spare, she arrived. She walked in and Jenny greeted her with a smile.

"Morning! I hope you're ready? Today is a big game!" There was a buzz in the air and preparations had already begun. Jenny whistled as she piled plates on the counter.

''Three points today. We need them,'' Jenny said, like a kid hoping for that special present from Santa at Christmas. Her fingers were crossed on both hands.

''Let's hope so,'' Keith replied, his focus not wavering from his cooking. The smell of bacon made her mouth water. A short girl was filling the coffee machine, standing unsteadily on a foot stall.

''Yes, I'll cry today if we don't get them,'' she responded and turned to Zara. "Hi, I'm Tina. Match days are manic and I'm glad we have extra hands. I can't help during the week because of University and poor Jen needs it. So, you ready?" Zara nodded and smiled.

They gave Zara her instructions, and the four of them worked hard. They bonded quickly, and by the time the team arrived for breakfast, everything was ready. Zara hoped Jake was on time. The players filed in and at the back looking relatively normal was Jake in his club tracksuit. The relief was instant as he spotted Zara and waved from the door. Their night's ordeal was over. When he approached a few minutes later, he leaned over to her.

''Are you okay?'' he whispered.

"I'm fine," she whispered back.

"I am sorry, truly sorry," his eyes locked on hers and she couldn't breakaway.

''I know. You know what I want as an apology?''
she handed him a plate. "Eat.''

''Yes, Gaffer. I'll do my best,'' he winked as he
walked away.

Jenny and Tina whistled from behind her. They
exchanged knowing looks between them. ''What
was that about?'' Jenny teased. ''What does he have
to say sorry for?''

They had heard enough to pick up on something.

''It's nothing,'' her mind raced for something to tell
the girls. ''He nearly drove into me yesterday, that's
all.'' It was the first thing that popped into her head.
Jenny and Tina seemed to accept it, but a not-so-
subtle look between them made her doubt it.

''He keeps looking over. I think you have an
admirer. Although, I'd be careful…his ex is a
nutter,'' Jenny warned.

''Oh, god. Ivy – fucking – Mason! I can't stand the
stuck-up bitch,'' Tina mumbled as she walked
away, shaking her head. Everyone knew about
Jake's ex-girlfriend. She was a fame-obsessed
swimsuit model with a temper and was always in
the press.

''He's better off without her,'' Jenny commented.
"She was in here a while back, causing trouble.
Poor Tina was only talking to him, and Ivy was

screaming and shouting. It was embarrassing. It wasn't long after that he ditched her. Best thing he's done in weeks. Poor lad couldn't do anything without her showing him up.''

Zara was glad he'd got rid of her. That's control. And she knew all about that behaviour.

''She's always got some drama going on?'' Zara asked.

''It's all PR for her,'' Tina snapped, returning with some dirty plates. ''Can't stand her. She's not remotely nice to anyone,'' Tina shuddered before disappearing into the back of the kitchen.

Once breakfast had ended and they'd prepped for lunch, the crew finally had a short time to eat. Tina went outside to smoke. Jenny frowned, she hated smoking.

''Do you smoke?'' Tina asked Zara.

''I gave up two years ago, but I vape sometimes. Mostly when I'm stressed.'' That morning she'd vaped on the way to work. Jake Maddox had caused her stress.

Jenny clapped her hands together, the sign it was time to get back to work. The fast pace of the job meant there was no time to get bored, which was a bonus. Everyone hoped for a win and the anticipation was in the air. In the kitchen, they could watch the match while serving the executive boxes. Their job didn't stop. Zara caught as much as she could and so far it was an even match. Although, no goals yet.

The roar of the crowd vibrated around the ground. As Zara arrived back at the kitchen, Jenny and Tina were watching the screen.

''Bloody Hell, Jake, what are you doing?!'' her boss raged at the screen. ''He looks like he's knackered.''

Zara couldn't disagree, he wasn't on form and she knew the reason. His pace was slow, and he had missed several open goals. She wouldn't get her Hat-Trick today. The second half was no better, and as the clock ticked to the eightieth minute, it got worse. Jake flew into a Tottenham player who was lucky to get back up. There was no other decision the referee would make. Everything slowed as the ref reached for his pocket. Zara closed her eyes in dread as she saw the flash of the red card. He and Jake argued causing chaos on the pitch. Hayden Palmer was furious and screamed in Jake's face telling him exactly what he thought of his actions. Ted showed no emotion, but he didn't look at Jake either as he trudged off with his head down. Behind the calm exterior, there was fury. The team fell to pieces after that, and they lost four-nil.

''Stupid idiot!'' Jenny raged, tears in her eyes. ''What's the matter with him, lately. It isn't like him.''

The happy vibe circulating the club before the game started had disappeared, and Zara hoped nobody found out what had happened. She feared for them both; him for being so irresponsible and her part in covering it up.

When the players arrived later to greet family and friends in the lounge, the mood was ice cold. Families made comforting comments to ease the disappointment, but it didn't work. The manager had a face of thunder. As expected, Jake was not popular, and eventually, it got heated between Jake and Ben Virgo. The goalkeeper glared at Jake from across the room. Zara didn't hear what sparked the bust-up, but Ben punched Jake in the face. The connection made a sickening sound, sending him flying over a table. Blood poured from his face, and the rest of the team had to pull them apart. But secretly, they all had wanted to do the same.

The day ended on a bitter note, and Zara was thankful when it was time to go home.

3

Zara sat at a traffic light, her mind going over the match and the aftermath. As much as Jake's behaviour was disgraceful, she couldn't help but think about him. She wanted to know if he was ok. Taking a risk, she headed to his house. Once she had checked on him, she knew she could relax. It could be a mistake, but she felt a need to do it anyway.

It was getting dark when she pulled up outside the large house. His car was in the drive and a few lights were on. Nervously, she stepped out of the car and approached the door. Knocking loudly, doubt crept in and she wondered if this was a bad idea.

It took a few minutes before the sound of the lock clicked and the door opened. Jake looked terrible. A bruise had formed on his cheek from Ben's angry punch, his lip was swollen, and he looked downcast.

''What do you want?'' he said, his voice low but not unkind.

''I came to see if you are okay?'' Zara said, ''Can I come in?''

He shrugged, sighed heavily, and let her step inside. ''If you're here to have a go, join the massive line of teammates, manager, press, and fans.''

He led her to a spacious lounge, kitted out with anything a twenty-something rich footballer would need. Expensive sofa, coffee table, TV, and Xbox. The walls were lined with football memorabilia, a few of his achievements, and pictures from players from the past.

''I'm not here to make you feel any worse than I'm sure you already do.''

''I didn't get the hat-trick I promised you.'' He leaned his head back and closed his eyes, "You won't get it in the next game either. I've a one-match ban after today.''

Zara sat next to him. ''Forget about that. You seemed so angry on the pitch...everyone says it's out of character for you.''

He wouldn't look at her.

''You were fine before the game. Did something happen after I saw you?'' He shook his head, but Zara didn't believe him. ''You can trust me.''

 ''I can't trust anyone,'' he laughed sarcastically. The anger was back. ''Nobody! I have all this, but I don't have trust in anyone. People just take, take, take. Jake will score all the time…Jake will cover it…well fucking Jake doesn't want to be the nice, reliable guy all the time.'' His hands were shaking.

''I just want to help, that's all,'' Zara meant every word.

''You can't help, but thanks.''

''I can listen,'' Zara said, her voice soft. This wasn't just about the red card. He was hiding something and for whatever reason, he couldn't or wouldn't tell her.

''It was a bad day. I feel terrible. I let everyone down. I'm awful to be around after a day like today,'' he murmured. ''Last night, that was selfish too. I need to put things right with everyone tomorrow.''

It was a good place to start. He settled a little, and she made them both strong coffees, and for the next hour they talked about everything but the match. Zara managed a smile from him.

"Won't Ivy be mad about me being here?'' Zara asked, well aware of his connection to the swimsuit model and her reputation of being vicious regarding him. He seemed annoyed at the mention of her name.

"It's none of her business who I have in my house. I ditched her weeks ago. She just won't take the fucking hint.'' Zara felt a sense of relief but wasn't sure if it was because she was safe from a raging girlfriend, or that he was single.

"Ivy was hard work and deranged. Plus, she was only with me for the clout, anyway. I'm done with her."

He was angry with her. That was certain. There was no love when he talked about her, only resentment. In that brief conversation, she saw a different person. A friendship was forming, and she welcomed it.

Finishing the coffee, Zara stood to leave.

"Do you have to go?'' Jake seemed disappointed as she prepared to leave.

"I should. You need to get some rest anyway," she smiled and opened the door. They hovered on his doorstep, an awkwardness between them. Not a bad one though. She could have stayed and talked to him all night if she wanted to be the next person in the gossip columns. But, she didn't, so leaving was the sensible move.

'Thanks for the coffee. Get some rest, Jake. You look tired,'' his blue eyes seemed dull, and his demeanour was low.

"Sure you can't stay?'' he asked, hope in his voice.

''I can't. But another time, maybe. Try not to beat yourself up too much.''

"You made it a little better. Thanks,'' he leaned down and kissed her softly on the cheek.

Inside the car, parked at a distance, the photographer smiled. A cigarette hung from his mouth as the shutter clicked ninety-seven times. Another perfect money shot. He rubbed his hands together. His collection was ready for the highest bid.

The drive home gave her time to think, and she liked the Jake she'd just spent the last few hours with. The realisation hit her, Jake Maddox had just kissed her. She knew it was only on the cheek. It meant nothing more than a friendly gesture, but she had to admit…it was nice.

This past week had exposed a different side to this industry, one you don't see from the stands on a Saturday. Zara had been guilty of the usual perception many had:

They get paid so much money. What do they have to worry about? They should just get on with it.

I guess to a point, she could agree. But they were also human, just like the rest of us. No amount of money can stop you from having a shocker, or make you win every week. A Striker cannot score every second they are on the pitch, nor can a goalkeeper save every attempt that rockets his way. It's impossible. Zara had bonded with these people. All who worked in this club, even Ted. She saw a man under pressure daily and that made her want to do the best job she could.

Success was what they strived for. Zara wouldn't be a star player on the pitch, but she could shine in her job.

Once she was finally home, she made pasta and fell asleep on the sofa after several glasses of wine. Today had been exhausting. When she woke later that evening, the TV was still blaring and the room was only lit up by the TV screen. Her phone had woken her, vibrating on the coffee table. It was one in the morning and the phone screen displayed a message from Jake.

Thanks for tonight.

The smile spread across her face, but she responded in a way Ted would be proud of.

Go to sleep Jake. Training in the morning and a lot of grovelling.

There was a brief delay before he responded.

Yes, Gaffer.

An emoji of rolling eyes next to the text.

4

Zara hung up her jacket and went to check what needed doing. Jenny usually greeted her, but the kitchen was empty. Her boss's coat and bag were there, but no Jenny. There was an eerie feeling. This was unusual. Concentrating on preparing breakfast while waiting for Jenny to appear felt like ages. It was twenty minutes later when a stern-looking Jenny stormed in. Her face pale, and she was pointing at Zara.

''Office now!'' she yelled. Zara followed, worried. The door slammed behind them once in Jenny's small office. ''What the hell have you done?''

''Me? Nothing. What's wrong?''

Her boss banged her hand down, making her jump.

''Don't lie, you can't lie when you are fooling around with Jake Maddox. I take it you've not seen today's news?'' Jenny threw several newspapers on the desk. Zara's stomach twisted into knots. Every newspaper or media outlet had a similar headline.

Maddox scores with clubs' new kitchen girl!

Kitchen Girl ruins star striker!

"Oh, fuck," Zara gasped. The pictures of her entering his house and leaving told the story all by themselves. Wrong, but who cares about that. It was the picture of her getting Jake out of the bar the night before the match, then him kissing her cheek. They were the pictures that condemned her.

Zara's mouth was dry. Thoughts buzzed around her head. This was her worst nightmare, come true.

"So, come on. What happened?' Jenny waited, one eyebrow cocked in irritation.

The hesitation had just made it worse. Zara's mind was moving in slow motion. She couldn't get her words out. They were a jumbled mess.

''I'm waiting!" Jenny screeched. "Do you know what's happening right now? There are furious people in this club."

''It really isn't what it looks like.'' Zara's voice sounded feeble, and Jenny's expression was stone cold.

"Bullshit. You were in his house for hours, alone, and you expect me to believe that? Jake was out the night before a game, smashed out of his face with you! He lost that game for us, and you said nothing. Now we are without him for the game against Everton. How stupid are you both?'' Jenny was irate.

''I was not out with Jake.''

Jenny picked up the papers again, shoving them in her face.

''Jenny, please listen. I was out with my friend and we saw him. I was trying to get him out of there.''

Jenny calmed as she processed her response, ''I wasn't happy with him either. He came back to mine and sobered up. Obviously, I underestimated the press.''

Zara told her boss everything. Jenny listened without interrupting.

''You promise that's the truth?'' Jenny questioned cautiously.

Zara nodded. ''Yes, I know it looks bad. But I was only trying to help. I didn't want him to be in trouble or the club to have bad press. Maybe I handled it wrong, but he's a grown-man and what he did that night had nothing to do with me. Last night, I went to check on him and he was low. He knows he screwed up.''

Jenny ran her hands through her red hair, sighing loudly.

''Bloody Hell. The gaffer is raging, and the Chief Executive is on the warpath. Jake is in Ted's office and I hope he backs up your story. It's like a pressure cooker in this club at the moment, and Ted doesn't need this drama.''

Zara's heart raced. ''I did nothing wrong.'' Tears flowed down her cheeks. ''Please don't fire me. I love this job.''

Jenny passed her some tissues and told her to dry her eyes.

"I was just trying to help,'' Zara pleaded.

''I'm not going to fire you. We still have football players that need feeding, so concentrate on the job. We can sort this out later. Tina has a day off from university today, she will be here soon. I called her when I heard what happened because I didn't know how this would pan out.''

The thought of facing people made Zara feel sick. There was nothing she could do but get on with her job.

''You're not sleeping with Jake?'' Jenny turned and asked suddenly. Zara shook her head.

''No.''

"You spent several hours in his house and just talked. So, he kissed you because nothing happened?"

"Yes. I think he just needed someone to talk to. It was just a friendly kiss. That's the truth.''

"Well, the country thinks otherwise."

A sense of relief that Jenny believed her gave Zara a bit of comfort. Although, convincing her was easier than the public jury. Then a text came through, and her stomach flipped.

Zara, what is going on? Jake Maddox! You're all over Twitter, babe. You went to his house? Call me! I want to know the details. OMG!!!

She put her head in her hands, knowing this was just the beginning. After a pep talk from Jenny and a large coffee, she tackled her work. Nothing took her mind off her situation. The phone rang and Jenny answered, ''Zara, it's Linda on reception.''

"Hey," the receptionist was whispering. "Listen carefully, there is press outside and they are waiting for you." She sounded concerned for her, but underneath it was also giving Linda a new point of gossip. ''You can't come out your usual way. And that's not all…''

Zara felt her throat dry up. ''What else could be worse than the press?''

''Jake's girlfriend,'' Linda whispered. ''She's on the warpath and she's out for blood. Your blood.''

Zara looked at the wall as the realisation of her situation became clear.

"Bollocks! Ivy?" Linda confirmed that the swimsuit model was the very one waiting for Zara to 'Show her slag face'.

''Wait, they broke up weeks ago?''

''It's Jake Maddox. Who knows who he's seeing, but Ivy seems to think you're stealing her man.''

'Wonderful. Thanks, Linda, for the heads up," Zara slammed the receiver down making Jenny jump.

"What!?' Jenny questioned.

"Ivy Mason," Zara said. Jenny rolled her eyes.

"Great PR opportunity for her. Although be careful, nasty piece of work, that one," Jenny warned, reminding Jenny of Ivy's temper.

Zara felt sick and rushed to the bathroom. Her phone had blown up. Family and friends were eager to know what was going on. The other numbers she didn't know wouldn't be well-wishers. She was sure of that.

Her solitary moment, locked in the cubicle, didn't last long enough.

"Hey, Zara, are you in here?'' Jenny's voice was soft and caring.

"No, I vanished in a cloud of smoke," Zara responded, hoping that would actually happen.

"If what you said is true, it'll be okay. But...!''

"Don't say 'But'...'' Zara pleaded, worry in her voice.

Jenny knocked on the door, "You need to come out. Ted wants to see you in his office.''

"Great!'' Zara said with sarcasm. "I wish I had shagged him. At least it would have been true.''

"You'll be fine. Best bet is to tell the truth. Ted knows a lie before you've opened your mouth."

It was true, and her only option was to get Ted on her side. It felt like the walk of shame as she approached the manager's door. Two knocks and a few seconds of silence before he invited her in. Ted didn't look up when she first entered, his attention focused on paperwork. He made a sound like a lion, a growl from his throat.

Do they think I came down in the last shower! Five million for Jamie? Fucking insulting," he shoved them to the side where Zara knew they'd stay. Even she knew Jamie Boxall was worth much more than that.

"Sit," Ted barked and used his hand to gesture to the opposite chair. "Zara, can you explain the mess I've woken up to?" Ted asked. He sat back in his chair and waited for her to answer.

"I just tried to help him. I wasn't out with him. I saw him in the bar and was trying to help." She repeated the story, hoping he would believe her. She hoped Jake had said the same.

Ted continued to stare at her calmly before leaning forward and tapping a newspaper.

"I can tell when a millionaire playboy footballer is lying. It's a gift I have, so you don't stand a chance."

"I'm not lying," Zara said defensively. Fear and shame, even though she'd done nothing wrong, swept over her. How did he do that?

"Zara, what you and Jake do in private is none of my concern, unless it affects the team and this club.''

"Nothing happened…we are not…" She blurted out like a naughty teenager caught out by her parents. Ted leaned forward, not breaking eye contact.

"I don't give a shit if you shagged him or not, but I don't take kindly to a player acting the idiot.'' The surrounding air switched. He played her just the same as anyone else.

"I'm sorry. Don't fire me. I love this job. I didn't mean to cause any trouble. He…'' she snapped her mouth shut before she said anymore. It was too late. Ted had already figured it out.

''He told you not to.''

''I didn't know what to do!'' her words fell out, she stumbled, and she knew she'd just added to Jake's troubles. "Oh, God. I'm so done here, I'll go.''

Ted laughed loudly.

''Zara, calm down. You're not getting fired. I believe you, and Jake told me the same thing. He said you had been a good friend, and you gave him a rollicking that I'd be proud of.'' Zara felt relief fill her.

"Zara, what you do with whoever isn't my concern. Just don't keep things from me about my players, ever. That's all I ask. I'm worried about Jake, but you seem to handle him well. He has been very honest, and I had a sincere apology, and I suspect you are the reason for that."

Zara explained how she'd reminded him of his responsibilities and how selfish he had been.

"Zara, I am impressed. I'd have loved to have seen his face!'' He roared with laughter. "Usually, the ladies hang on his every word.''

"I'm not the usual girl. If you act like an idiot, I'll tell you. Famous or not.'' Ted laughed again and Zara asked, ''Are all footballers such hard work?''

"You've seen nothing…believe me. They can be much worse.'' That was not comforting, but she liked a challenge.

''I don't know how to handle the press thing. I didn't think I would have to." He must have seen the trepidation in her expression. "I don't want to do anything else to cause any more trouble.''

"Say absolutely nothing," he replied without hesitation. "They don't care about the truth. Jake can handle it. He likes you, so you'll be fine. Don't worry about the press, I will sort that lot out.'' He flicked his head toward the vultures. "Oh, and I'll deal with Miss Mason too."

 Zara knew he would protect her and the team. "I've never understood the fuss about players and their love affairs, but people thrive off it. People are obsessed with these men and want to know what it would take for them to have a chance. Jake is like jumping into a shark-infested ocean for any woman.''

"The kiss on the cheek was nothing. I helped him, that's all.''

"A kiss on the cheek by Jake Maddox to those idiots is hardly nothing."

Zara smiled and felt a newfound respect for Ted and all he had to endure to keep the players and the team in order.

 "Now get to work," Ted winked and nodded to the door.

As she left, she heard him call security, "Please remove Miss Mason from the premises. I won't have my staff threatened and remind her she is no longer with Jake Maddox. She has no business being here. And keep those nosey bastards out of this club!"

Zara held back from punching the air. Her day passed quickly. The players were offish but didn't say too much. She figured they'd been told to keep out of it.

5

The carpark was almost empty as she headed to her car. It wasn't until she approached the exit she remembered Linda's warning call. The cluster of people outside the club was waiting to get a glimpse of her. There was no point in changing direction, they'd spotted her. Taking a deep breath, she drove on.

Ted's words were loud in her head. "Say absolutely nothing," which she repeated over and over in her head.

The exit from the carpark was suddenly a very daunting place. The security guard at the entrance saw her approach, and the gates opened.

"Are you okay going out there?" he asked.

Zara nodded, but she had never felt so vulnerable, and it was unnerving. The image of Jake's ex-girlfriend popped into her mind. That woman made her confidence drop. At least she hadn't hung around making the experience even worse. Zara thought about the night before. Jake Maddox had flipped her life with an unauthorised night out, a red card, and an innocent kiss on the cheek. It was ridiculous that people thought Jake would go for her…not that he would go for her. She wasn't sure she even wanted him to. She didn't know what she wanted.

Her car exited and camera lenses pointed at her like a SWAT team. Holding her nerve, she put on a confident look. Just a girl driving out of a carpark. Then the shouts began:

"Zara, how long have you been dating Jake?''

"Did you steal him from Ivy?''

"Do you feel responsible for the loss on Saturday?''

"Are you embarrassed by both of your actions?''

"The fans deserve an apology, you and Jake showed no respect!"

"Turns out Jake likes a bit of the rough.'' That comment stung, but she didn't react.

"Say absolutely nothing.'' Ted's words were her lifeline through that terrifying moment. They swarmed the car as she slowed. Panic rose, but she didn't show it. Her foot hovered over the accelerator as the engine ticked over. Zara focused on the road ahead, waiting for a moment to flee. It felt like being caged in a zoo. Then, as she was about to lose her control and burst into tears, something distracted the pack. A loud rev of an engine made her look up. The black car approached, and they slammed the breaks on. It came to a halt. The door opened, and Jake jumped out, his sunglasses shielding his eyes.

"Get away from her!'' he yelled, marching towards the mellay. "I said move!''

He ignored the cameras aimed at him. Obviously, they didn't bother him. He approached her passenger side and got in. His movement was quick.

"I need to get you out of here. Come with me.''

"My car!'' Zara cried.

"Don't worry about your car.'' Now they were both trapped. "When I say get out, run to my car and get in. And whatever they say or do…"

"Say nothing,'' she finished the sentence for him. He smiled, "You learn quickly. Ready?'' Zara nodded.

"Now!'' Jake said, and she shut off any thought that would stop her. The door hit a few photographers as it swung open. Head down, she pushed her way through the crowd. A hand grabbed hers and steered her around the bonnet, and they were running. The doors of his car opened, and she threw herself in. Jake was beside her seconds later. He slammed the car into reverse, spun it 'round, and they made their escape.

"Are you ok?'' Jake asked once they were at a safe distance to relax.

"No! What the fuck was that?''

"Welcome to my world,'' he said, sounding more at ease now that the crowd was behind them.

"Don't they have a life?''

Jake chuckled. ''People like me are their life and that kiss on the cheek would have paid the nosey little prick a lot of money.'' Zara slumped back against the leather seat.

"Thanks, I didn't know what to do,'' she said, feeling overwhelmed.

"You're welcome,'' he responded. "It was the least I could do…it's my fault it happened.'' His eyes flicked to look at her.

"Seatbelt," he commanded. Zara grabbed for it and snapped it in place. "Last thing I want is you going through the windscreen." He checked his mirror, "They're behind us."

"How do you know?" Zara asked, turning around to look out the rear window.

"I know…trust me," he activated his phone using voice. "Call Virgo." After two rings, Ben answered.

"Maddox, what a performance. You and Zara were live on TV!" Ben roared with laughter. "What do you need, mate?" The tension from the last game had vanished, and they seemed friendly again.

"Zara needs help, and your place has more security than Buckingham Palace. Just until these pricks get bored." There was a silence before Ben Virgo laughed loudly, "For fuck's sake, the kids are running riot, and the wife's about to lose her shit with them, so it's a madhouse here. If she likes madhouses, she's welcome."

Horror filled Zara. "I can't just turn up at his house. It's not his problem!" There was a pause before a female voice took over.

"Zara, if you can handle a house full of football-obsessed boys, you are welcome." Ben's wife sounded friendly, funny, and welcoming.

"If you're sure?''

"Get over here. I'll open the wine. Bloody boys.'' There was another pause and then a shout, "James, not in the house! No football in the house!'' The phone cut off.

"I'm confused,'' Zara said, still perplexed by the phone call.

"About what?''

"Why call Ben? He punched you in the face.''

Jake laughed and checked his mirrors once more. "I got a red card. We lost. It pissed him off,'' Jake said, shrugging. Zara stared at him, her mouth open in disbelief.

"But. But. He punched you in the face.''

"What happened yesterday is nothing, you should see us when it really kicks off. He called after you left last night. We sorted it out. It happens all the time,'' he laughed at a memory. "The stories I could tell…''

Zara's thoughts reverted to their current situation. "Why were you even there?'' His expression didn't change. "At the club, I mean. Training finished hours ago.'' Jake smiled at her question.

"I knew they would go for you when you left. I also know when you usually leave.'' Again, he'd thrown her. He'd deliberately come to the club to help her.

"You came to save me then?''

"I guess so. Look I'm used to this and I know how they work. It's brutal. You don't deserve that.''

"But…haven't your heroics just given them what they want?''

"Yep,'' he nodded. "I couldn't just leave you to the wolves.'' He stopped talking and concentrated on driving.

Zara could feel the tears pricking at her eyes. She thought she would've' handled the press better…know what to do. They had proven her wrong.

"Don't let them get to you, it's what they want,'' Jake said as if he'd read her mind.

"One said something that hurt, that's all. I don't want to cause you any trouble or embarrassment.''

He took a sharp turn onto a narrow country road. After a slow and bumpy ride, and Jake cursing each time his car hit a hole, they arrived at their destination. The country house sat back surrounded by an impressive security gate. Ben Virgo's home stood before us and it was beautiful. Jake tapped his phone as they approached and without having to stop, the gates opened. As the gates closed, Zara let out a sigh of relief.

"Embarrassment?'' he asked.

"It doesn't matter. It was just stupid comments. I know they do that for a reaction.''

"What did they say?'' Jake sounded irritated. ''Like I can't guess.''

"Just…'' she wished she'd kept her mouth shut. "That it seems you go for a bit of rough now. I'm not glamorous enough, they seem to think.''

He snapped off his seat belt and turned to look at her, "Do I look embarrassed?''

"No.'' Zara wanted the ground to open and devour her. This was intense.

"The press are like bloodhounds, one sniff and they attack,'' he smiled at her. "Don't worry, it'll be okay. Come on, let's get inside.''

6

Zara followed him to the front door. It opened and two boys came running out.

"Jake, come and play football!'' Jake patted the boy on the head. He was around eight years old and fitted out in a goalkeeper kit. Just like his dad. A younger boy, roughly three years old, ran to him. Jake picked him up and hugged him.

"Give me ten minutes, James, and you can show me how much better you are than your dad.'' This made the boy cheer, and he ran back into the house.

"Todd, dude, you are getting big,'' the small boy threw his arms around Jake and held on tight. ''Football…play,'' he said, Zara's heart melted at the adorable child. He turned, noticing Zara. "Who?'' he said.

"This is my..." he paused, thinking about how he would introduce her. "my friend. Her name is Zara. She works with your Daddy and me."

The boy lost interest in her and struggled to get down. He pulled Jake by the hand into the house.

"Jake, lovely to see you," Jenna Virgo said as she hugged him. Ben's wife was much shorter than she seemed in the papers. She looked exhausted but still pretty in a more natural, subtle way. She wore no make-up and wore gym wear. Her long black hair pulled tightly back into a ponytail.

"Hey, Jenna. Where is he then?"

Jenna ignored the question and checked Jake's face, "Hmm, didn't hit you hard enough, I see." She giggled, "He's in the garden. James broke the goal, again. He also smashed a crystal vase by doing penalties in the goddam lounge."

Her gaze moved to Zara, her head tilted. "Don't listen to anything or read anything," she said, then took Zara by the arm and guided her into the spectacular kitchen. Zara liked her instantly. Jenna had two glasses of sparkling wine ready for them and guided her out onto the large garden patio. Ben waved from the bottom of the garden.

"Zara, you ran faster than Jake...gave him a run for his money." Ben laughed. Zara glanced at Jenna, her eyes wide.

"Oh, it's already on BBC news. The rescue of Zara Rose.'' She pushed a glass of wine towards Zara. "Don't worry about it. Get used to it. If you want to date Jake, it's part of the deal.'' Jenna was so calm and to the point, but she had it all wrong.

"I'm not dating Jake. None of this is what it seems. Why won't people believe me?'' Zara sighed.

Jenna leaned back in her chair and pushed her sunglasses to the top of her head. Her emerald green eyes were full of knowledge.

"I know you're not dating Jake…yet,'' she took a sip of her wine and shouted down towards her husband, Jake, and her boys. ''Don't break it again, and James no more penalties in the house.''

Ben lifted his hand, "Yes Boss.'' Zara looked between the two and saw the complete love that flowed between them.

"I don't think that will happen. He was just helping me out. It's just so crazy how the country has decided my life. I don't even know what I am doing with my life.'' Zara took her glass and drained it. She needed that. Jenna chuckled.

"Damn girl! Another?'' Zara nodded and relaxed a little. Jake had been right about one thing. She was safe here. Nobody was getting in this house. She watched as the game of football played out. Todd tripping over his tiny feet. Ben deliberately allowing him to score. The little boy running to Jake, seeking his approval.

''Outstanding shot kid!'' Jake called.

"Jake should move and find a better place to live,'' Jenna said. "I keep telling him. When Ben and I moved here, it was the best thing we ever did. I know how it is, I've been there. God, I remember pulling away from Ben because of the press. They nearly destroyed me. I ended our engagement because I couldn't cope with it.''

Jenna opened up about all she'd been through. Some of it Zara knew about from reading the papers, but this was her chance to hear it from the women herself. She wanted to know if the stuff in the papers had been true.

"Did he do what they accused him of?'' she braved the question. Sadness spread across the face of the goalkeeper's wife.

"No. He would never do that. That girl even admitted to me she'd done it out of spite, but that didn't get printed. Yes, he cheated. I never denied that, and he didn't either. But... hitting a woman. No way. It broke my heart to deal with the cheating and then that. I believed that bitch at first and hated him because of her.''

If Jenna was trying to make her feel better about dating a footballer, she had just failed. Zara was more terrified. "Why did you take him back?''

"Because there was so much more to the story. Reasons, he strayed. I knew the real Ben. He hated what he did, and he did everything in his power to make it right. I wasn't perfect either at the beginning of our relationship. We were young, it was ten years ago. We realised we were stronger together. Ben would never hit a woman, never."

"Do you trust him?'' Zara asked, intrigued by Jenna Virgo. There was no hesitation before she answered.

"With my life.''

"Why did that woman lie?'' Zara continued to prod.

"Because they hooked up once, a one-night stand. We were not getting on. He thought things wouldn't get better between us. I got over my tantrum a few days later, and he came running back. She didn't like it. She had the sodding wedding planned in her head. Delusional bitch."

Jenna had held this in for a long time, that was clear, and Zara listened.

"I understood it hurt her. That I don't begrudge. Men don't understand how women get so swept up in moments like that, but to injure her own face and blame him. She nearly ended his career!'' Jenna was crying now. ''It devastated him. Ok, he might get a bit carried away, like the other day during the match. That's football. But strike a woman…he wouldn't Zara. He just wouldn't.''

Zara felt a sense of common ground. Even though she wasn't dating anyone, the press and the public had decided otherwise. "Two days ago my life was uneventful, and then…"

"Jake happened.'' Jenna finished.

"Yeah, Jake. And within forty-eight hours, I almost killed a sixty-five million pound Spanish footballer, pissed off the manager, and become front-page news for dating Jake Maddox even though I'm not. I'm living the dream.'' Both women looked at each other and burst into laughter.

"Never a dull moment in football!'' Jenna gasped between bouts of laughter. ''If I were you, I'd run. Run!''

"I would but…''

"Jake?'' Janna asked.

"No, I don't know where the hell I am, and my car is still at the club!'' This caused more hysterical laughter.

From the bottom of the garden, Jake watched with a smile on his face. Ben's voice broke his trance.

"If you want my advice, I'd make it work. She's perfect for you.'' He was serious, no jokes this time. "You have been with some stunning women, but you've never been happy. The way you protected her today, you've never done that with anyone else. She isn't Ivy Mason, but that girl right there is beautiful inside and out. Plus, she knows this industry and loves the game. It's a perfect match.''

"They made vicious comments about her,'' Jake answered. ''That she's not glamourous enough.'' Ben picked up on his tone sensing Jake wasn't in agreement. "I can't put her through that crap.''

"They said the same things about Jenna. Did I give a shit? My wife is a fucking goddess. Out of all those I dated, she was my soul mate, she loved me. Not this!'' He pulled his wallet out of his pocket. "When I nearly lost everything. It was Jenna that was by my side. Even after that bitch ran my name through the mud because I wouldn't marry her.'' Ben spoke with a fierceness. He worshipped his wife and god help anyone who went near her. "Ivy just wants the fame.''

"I know,'' Jake replied. ''If anyone truly knew you, they'd have known you'd never have raised a hand to a woman.''

Ben shrugged, "People love a villain.''

Jake remembered it well. It had almost destroyed his friend. Luckily, there was evidence on the girl's phone proving she'd lied.

"I just think it would be selfish of me. Ivy wants all the attention. Zara doesn't. The best thing for me to do is leave her alone." Jake rarely thought that way. If he wanted someone, he usually got them. Zara was different.

Ben looked at him, a sceptical look on his face. "You? Not go for the girl!?" He shook his head. "I'll bet a week's wages you won't last the week."

Jake didn't respond. He wouldn't take that bet. Ben would more than likely win. If he was honest, it was hard just being there with her, sitting there looking so innocently stunning. She didn't even realise how lovely she was, feisty but honest. She hadn't once asked about money or who he knew, a breath of fresh air in his experience. He could just walk over to her and kiss her, and more if she let him. His thoughts went to an erotic place, and he knew it would be hard to keep away.

"Earth to Maddox!" Ben yelled in his ear. He sniggered. "Man, you won't last the week. You can't even stop looking at her."

"Shut it!" he snapped. "Can you get her home?"

"I'll call Brian, he will sort it." Brian was the player liaison officer. He was the club's keeper of secrets. If anyone could get Zara home undetected, he could.

"You're staying though, you don't just drop off your secrets at my door and run." Jake booted the ball at Ben, a powerful shot full of anger and frustration. Jake Maddox for the first time in his life would put the needs of someone else before himself. Ben knew his teammate would struggle And, he was confident that he was right this time. The only difference was Jake would do the chasing this time.

As Jenna attended to Todd from falling and cutting his knee, Zara checked her emails. Without thinking, she opened her Twitter account. Something she regretted. Pictures of her and Jake leaving the bar, and Zara leaving his house. The comments were nasty, bullying, and confidence destroying:

Who is this girl?!

Jake has hit rock bottom going for her. Ivy Mason is much better looking.

Disgraceful she doesn't care about his career and he is letting her destroy it. Gold digger!

Bitch stole Ivy's man!

Another gold digger out for what she can get. That red card was embarrassing. Drop her if she's done this much damage in a brief space of time. The Club is trying to stay up and Jake acts like this.

There was much worse. Before shutting down her phone. She saw a post by Ivy Mason:

I'm heartbroken. I can't believe after all I've done for him. Zara Rose is a man stealing bitch!

The outpouring of support for her was sickening.

The act of hiding what she'd seen was hard. But she promised herself she would not cave in to them. They would not break her. Zara logged out and didn't read any further. As it turned into late evening, they ate dinner with Ben and his family. Jake kept his distance from Zara, she'd noticed his change in behaviour. He spoke if she spoke to him, but never unprompted. He didn't look in her direction, and even Jenna had picked up on it. Zara helped Jenna clear up the plates, trying hard to bury the feeling of hurt. After the onslaught online, his actions had just cut deeper.

"I'll find out from Ben what they were talking about. I know you keep saying nothing is going on, but there is something between you now. You're confused by his actions today. Racing to your defence, then giving the cold shoulder. I've seen this before, I have my theories on this. One thing I know for certain is, it isn't you. It's complicated. They place Jake on this pedestal. You're just…"

"too ugly for him," Zara snapped. "I get it. I'm not Ivy."

"No!" Jenna protested. "That's not what I meant." Jenna crossed her arms. "What has really upset you?" Zara's eyes teared up, and they flowed down her cheeks. "I read the comments on Twitter."

Jenna rolled her eyes, "Ahh, and everyone has an opinion and few are nice, right?" Zara nodded. "Don't let it upset you."

Zara had never looked at herself and hated her long ash-blonde hair or her honey-coloured eyes. Her shape was an hourglass. She had curves, but she'd always loved them. Her size ten had never bothered her. Today, for a moment, she questioned every part of her. Ivy was stunning, with perfect blonde hair, never out of place. She seemed flawless with a body any girl dreamed of. It was like looking at a princess doll.

"I hate that I let it get to me. I thought I was stronger. Why are they being so cruel? Ivy is slagging me off all over Twitter. It's like he cheated, but he hasn't, not with me anyway. As if he'd go for me."

After putting herself back together after her past relationship, she didn't want to be in that place again. Zara was the punching bag for trying to help. A decision that had backfired on her. Part of her wished she'd stayed out of it.

"It gets to everyone. Don't beat yourself up,'' Jenna smiled at her. "Take no notice of Ivy, she has always been the same.'' Jenna gave her a tight hug. "It will pass. Next week it will be someone else. Ride it out. People forget you're a human being. They sit hidden and spew hate and think it's ok. Easy to say just ignore it, but I've been there and it hurts. I think that's why Jake is keeping his distance. He knows how bad this can get. If he keeps his distance, they will eventually leave you alone. If he walks out on Saturday and scores, he will be a hero again. Unfortunately, it doesn't work the same for us. And stop putting yourself down! You are gorgeous!'' The door opened, disturbing their conversation. Ben held some glasses and Jenna took them.

"Zara, I've arranged a lift home for you. Brian will be here soon,'' Ben said. ''Everything okay in here?'' He looked between Zara and his wife. A subtle look made him retreat.

"Thank you,'' Zara said, giving a delicate smile.

"Anytime. You'll be all right. You have us to look out for you,'' he assured her. Jenna waved him away, and he took the hint.

"Take my number and call me if you need anything.'' Jenna saved her number on Zara's phone under the name Marie, her middle name.

69

"Thank you.'' Zara hoped she wouldn't need to, but she liked Jenna and, having her as a friend made her feel at ease. Jake stepped into the kitchen, his coat on and his car keys in his hand.

"Brian won't be long. I'm going to go, it's best if I leave first. I'll see you tomorrow,'' he said, and he held her gaze for a few seconds before turning away.

"Thanks,'' Jake was already outside and didn't hear her. Zara knew that was the end of their brief encounter. She'd hoped for more, tried to pretend it wasn't what she wanted, but in reality, it was. How can a heart break over something that never was?

"I've caused trouble for him. I didn't mean to,'' Zara said turning to Jenna.

"It's not your fault. Jake can handle himself. He's used to the attention. He knows what he's doing.''

Ben opened the door ten minutes later. "Your chariot awaits.''

7

It was an awkward drive home. Brian was a nice man, late forties at a guess. He said little, but he made her feel safe in his company. This was normal for him, and he did it to perfection.

"They followed Jake, so you have nothing to worry about," Brain assured her. "It's why Jake left first. He made sure they followed him."

Brian pulled up to Zara's flat and smiled, "Get yourself inside."

"Thank you," Zara said and ran to her flat. At the top of the stairs she halted, a figure stood by her door at the end of the hall. The dark shadow didn't move, making it more sinister. The smoke from his cigarette lingered above his head. In their hand was a metal bar. He tapped it against her door, a threatening sound.

"What do you want?!'' Her words came out more aggressive than she'd meant.

"Your boyfriend,'' the voice had a northern twang to it.

"I don't have a boyfriend,'' Zara snapped. "You have me mistaken.''

"Zara Rose?'' She didn't answer. "I'll take that as a yes.'' He sniggered. "Tell him we are watching.''

"Might help if I knew who you are talking about.'' She knew she shouldn't provoke, but her fiery side had rushed to the surface, and she was in defence mode. "Or better still, tell whoever it is yourself. I don't have a boyfriend.'' The bar smashed off the door. It was a warning.

"Oh, you do have an attitude. Don't be a silly girl and tell him we mean business, so do as we ask and nobody gets hurt.''

He laughed a low chuckle before lifting the weapon and resting it on his shoulder. He walked casually towards her, stopped and, held the metal bar out, close to her face. She saw it was a golf club.

"Boyfriend or not. He does as he's told, or we might have to change that pretty face of yours. That would be a real shame.''

A scarf covered his face and on his head was a black cap. The only thing she could see was his dark brown eyes. She stayed still until he was out of sight, and the sound of footsteps descending the stairs faded away into silence. Frantically searching for her keys in her coat pocket, she ran to her door and barricaded herself inside. Feeling vulnerable and scared, she wondered what to do? Jenna, she'd help but as she reached for her phone, a thought filled her mind. Jake was in serious trouble. She couldn't bring Ben and Jenna into this until she knew more. Whatever this was, she was now a target.

After a sleepless night, the sunlight warmed her bedroom. It didn't brighten her mood, though. Nothing could shake the memory of last night, and she had to wait for an Uber to arrive to take her to work. Brian had assured her security had put her car safely in the club carpark. They'd had to push it as she'd taken her key during the escape. At least getting home would be easier. The Uber driver knew who she was, but she held her own.

"Bit wrong, you having to get a taxi when that boyfriend of yours has a nice flash car,'' he laughed at himself. Zara said nothing. What was the point? ''Oh, had a row have we?''

" I'm going to be late, and I'm not in the mood,'' she snapped.

"Got ya. You'll be there soon, Miss Rose.''

He said nothing more during the journey. He'd think she was a stuck-up bitch, but at that moment she couldn't care less. The club loomed in front of them, and the joy she used to feel had vanished. Her parents and Rachel had been calling constantly, but she didn't know what to say to them, and her excuses to not talk were running out. At least being in the Uber would disguise her arrival. She felt better once inside the club grounds, safely behind the security gates.

"Hola!'' Alvaro shouted. He waved as he got out of his Aston Martin. That made her feel better.

"Hola,'' she responded. He walked with her. His English was getting better, but he still struggled with words. Although, he was friendly and willing to try.

"I walk you, inside. Yes? English press, not good. I protect you. Even if you nearly kill me,'' he took her arm, and she laughed.

"Thank you.''

"It's not a problem,'' Alvaro said. Zara noticed he was in his training gear, his black hair pulled back into a ponytail. He must have been nearly six feet. He made her look tiny.

"I will confuse them,'' He smiled cheekily. "Who are you sleeping with? Jake or me!'' His head went back as he laughed.

"Alvaro!" Zara said, panic in her eyes. "No, everyone hates me already!"

"No, I don't think they hate you. They envy you. That is all," he said confidently. "Come inside and away from these…" he waved his hand toward the waiting press. "Anyway, I have a girlfriend."

"People think I'm to blame for Jake's bad form. I'd stay away from me if I was you."

Álvaro made a disgusted sound and shrugged his shoulders, "Jake is a grown man. Only himself to blame. I do what I want. I can talk to anyone I feel like. My girlfriend knows I'm an honest man. She is a smart woman." He looked at her, searching her face, "You are with Jake?"

Zara shook her head.

"So, it's no problem." Zara didn't answer.

"Not with Jake, but maybe you'd like to?" He wasn't being nosey, he was genuinely interested.

"Honestly, I don't know what Jake and I are? Friends at the moment," she realised she was discussing her love life with a very famous Spanish Footballer. How her life had changed in a week, a complete switch in dynamics. It was exciting and terrifying all at the same time.

"I think Jake needs a girl like you."

"Thanks, I'll take that as a compliment. But…do I need a guy like Jake?'' Álvaro laughed loudly.

"This is a good point,'' he said walking away, still laughing. He turned back to her. ''Smart Miss Rose.''

Zara headed to the kitchen. Jenny was waiting with a suspicious look on her face.

"What were you and Álvaro chatting about?''

"Oh, for god's sake. I can't do anything around her without being interrogated,'' Zara snapped. "I'm sick of it.''

Jenny folded her arms, "Calm down, don't get your knickers in a twist.'' Her expression made Zara regret her outburst. "I was just asking.''

"Sorry. I'm a little on edge today. He was just making sure I was okay, that's all.''

"That's nice. Are you alright?'' Jenny asked. "I saw the great escape.'' Hiding her smile was difficult. ''It was epic.''

Jenny assured her there was no judgment. They were a team and would support each other. Having a warm feeling from everyone in the club had eased her worries. It was almost easy to forget about her encounter with the faceless visitor. But, she knew it wouldn't disappear and she had to face it. The morning passed quickly, banter flew around and nobody made her feel guilty.

"You have nothing to worry about," Jenny said during a quick break. "Everyone knows the press are a bunch of shits. They all have their times in the news. It's part of life in this industry. Although rarely a kitchen girl makes the front page."

The one person missing from that morning was Jake. He hadn't been in for his usual breakfast. She hoped there was a reason other than he was avoiding her. Surely that was not the reason, but her paranoia was at its peak. Morning turned into late afternoon. They had been so busy feeding players and catering for an important board meeting, there had been little time to think about anything else. Zara preferred having her mind kept busy. It helped to keep any anxiety under control. Once she had time to think, it would play havoc. At four in the afternoon, Jenny headed off to collect the dishes, cutlery, and mugs from around the club. She left Zara to clean down the kitchen. The radio played loudly, and she sang as she cleaned. A cough behind her made her spin around. Jake stood in the doorway, a smirk on his face.

"Don't stop on my account," he said, a warm smile spread across his face. Zara stopped, embarrassed.

"Jake."

"I wanted to check you got home okay?"

Zara hesitated. "Yes, but…'' she paused and looked at the floor. Jake took a step into the kitchen.

"What's wrong?" he asked with concern.

Eventually, she looked up at him, "What have you got yourself into?'' Jake tried to look innocent.

"Don't lie. I had a visitor last night at my flat. They had a message for you, and they threatened me.''

Jake looked panicked. "What?!''

"I think you better talk, now,'' Zara replied in a shaky voice. The colour drained from Jake's face.

"Fuck!'' Jake's fists clenched. "I'm sorry. I never wanted you involved in this,'' he turned away, unable to look at her.

"Talk to me. Please, Jake,'' her hand took his and pulled him towards her. "Look at me.'' He did as she asked with guilt in his eyes. His forehead pressed against hers. "Stay away from me, Zara. I'm no good for you.''

"Why? You don't like me?'' He shook his head.

"No. I mean yes. I do like you. It's just better for you,'' he sighed. "Just stay away.''

"Let me help,'' Zara begged.

"You can't. I can't tell you…I just can't."

"Why?" Zara snapped. "I'm involved now."

"Zara, please listen to me. If you think being with me is all fame and glamour, it isn't."

 Zara's eyes were wide, shocked at his assumption that his fame interested her.

"I don't give a shit how famous you are! They threatened me because of you. The world is attacking me because of you. I'm not angry, I am worried about you!" Jake said nothing, instead, he placed his hand on her face. He wiped the tear from her eye. It felt completely normal for him to do that. She should be angry, but she wasn't. He needed her, even if he wouldn't admit it.

''Please talk to me,'' she pleaded.

Jake didn't have time to answer. The door opened, and they stepped away from each other. Ben eyed them suspiciously.

 "Did I interrupt something?" he was still in his kit, mud all over him. He'd been doing extra training and hadn't showered yet.

"I'm just making sure she got home okay, that's all," Jake replied.

Ben walked to the coffee machine and got an extra-strong coffee. A suspicious look on his face. "Right," he said then took a sip of his drink. Whatever he was thinking, he kept to himself.

"Bloody kids would not sleep last night. I'm shattered," he complained. "I swear, they do it to punish me. By the way, Jenna wants to invite you both to dinner at the weekend, if you're free?"

Jake looked at Zara, waiting for her response.

"I'd love to. Saturday night is good for me." Hopefully, after a win, Zara thought. Ben and Jake would be in good moods.

Jake hesitated. "Yeah, why not? Thanks, mate."

Zara turned to Ben. "What time?"

"I'll check with Jenna and let you know," he threw his coffee cup in the bin, saluted, and left.

Zara liked Ben a lot. His genuine personality was so different compared to how he acted on the pitch. He was always shouting at his defenders and always looked angry. Off it, he was one of the friendliest people in the club. The contrast in all the players off the pitch was so different. Their desire to win took over during a match, it was all they cared about. Alvaro, for instance, people called him arrogant, selfish and, didn't think of others. He had proven to her that was untrue. Ben's past problems couldn't be further from the truth. And Jake was not what Zara had expected. Although, she was still trying to figure him out. The press implied there was unrest in the dressing room. There was none that she could see. And Ted, he was a man you didn't cross, but he wasn't unfair. If you worked hard, he gave respect where it was due. If you crossed him, you knew about it.

She had settled into this club easily. Her loyalty was more than just a fan now. It was stronger since she knew the players in person and she felt protective. She understood Jenny more than ever.

" I guess I will see you there?'' Zara said.

"Looking forward to it,'' Jake said, turning and walking away. The moment between them seemed distant now.

The week passed, and with Jake unavailable for the Everton game, she could relax. The crowd was louder than usual. They sang with passion, cheering the team on. Billy Fox netted an early goal, and a few minutes later Luka Babić, who was on instead of Jake, netted another. They were two-nil up after twenty minutes. The stadium was jumping, and Zara could celebrate for real this time. It was great to enjoy the game. Jake was at home, watching on his own. His message came through to her, as happy as everyone else. A thrill vibrated through her. He'd texted her seconds after the goal. She was the one he'd wanted to talk to about the game. That made her smile.

"Absolute fucking beauties. I want to be back to normal. I want to back out there."

"You will. We will fix this, whatever it is," she promised.

The first half ended with the same score. The team was dominating the game. Jenny had tears in her eyes. They buzzed around the kitchen and served with smiles on their faces. Zara left the kitchen and made her way towards the dressing rooms to check on water supplies for the next delivery. There was a commotion coming from the direction of the tunnel. The sound of boots heading away from the pitch. Jamie Boxall, the club's brick of a defender, came flying 'round the corner. His face was pale and he looked panicked. He was still in full kit and he stopped for nobody. Brian followed behind, "I'll drive, you can't in this state. I'll get you to the hospital."

It wasn't until after the game they received the terrible news. A car had hit his six-year-old daughter outside of their home. Her mother had been on the phone when she'd snuck out the front door. Everyone prayed she would pull through. After a much-needed, comfortable win, it had ended in tragedy.

Thankfully, a few days later they received the news. Rosie Boxall would make a full recovery. A broken arm, concussion, cuts, and bruises, but there was no lasting damage. She would be home by the end of the week.

8

Saturdays' game was Chelsea away. All focus was on winning. Three points were all that was on every player's mind. Zara travelled to all away games along with Jenny. Overseeing all food, they set the room booked for the team to eat in private away from other hotel guests with precision. Victor Collins, club executive, demanded it that way. Blake Treviño took over three years ago, a multibillionaire from New York. He rarely appeared at the club. He used Victor to run things, who Zara had only met once, and Blake, never. The team arrived, hungry as normal. Hayden made his presence known, already telling the team to "Dig deep" and "Three fucking points today, lads!" Before tucking into his breakfast. He homed in on Jake.

"You ready, Mads?'' his tone was stern, to the point. Jake nodded. "Good, we need your magic back.''

Billy Fox stood looking at the food, undecided on his choice.

"Zara, if you're single, maybe after the game we could...'' A voice cut him off.

"Foxy, stop thinking about getting your cock wet and sit the fuck down,'' Hayden could see what he was doing. In a deliberate attempt to wind Jake up, all eyes were on him. Zara hid her embarrassment.

"I'm just kidding,'' he smirked as he headed to his seat.

"Mind on the game. Fucking idiot.''

Ted didn't have to worry with Hayden as captain, he took no bullshit.

"All you've done is get on my fucking nerves. Shut the fuck up and eat!'' he winked in her direction. She mouthed "Thank you.''

Billy was the lovable rogue, the wind-up merchant who thrived off the banter. He didn't mean any actual harm but needed to learn to reign it in. He never knew when to stop. It got him into trouble a lot. Jake didn't take the bait. He quietly ate his breakfast and smiled across the room at her when nobody else was paying attention. A few hours later, it was time for them to leave. The hotel was only a few minutes from Stamford bridge. The team was preparing to get on the bus when Ted approached.

"Zara, where is he?'' Ted snapped. His tone made nerves stand on end.

Jenny stepped in between them, ''Ted, calm down. What's the problem?''

"Jake has vanished. Nobody can find him. It seems this one…" he pointed at Zara, "is the only one who he talks to lately.''

Jenny turned to look at her. ''Do you know where Jake is?''

"No. I saw him at breakfast with the rest of the team. I didn't speak to him.'' Her boss nodded. She believed her.

"That's right, Ted. She hasn't stopped today. If Jake has taken off, it is nothing to do with Zara. I believe she would tell you if she knew something,'' she looked at her, wanting assurance she was telling the truth.

"I have no idea where he is,'' Zara replied.

Ted seemed to accept her answer. He calmed and politely asked, "Can you see if you can track him down. Please? He won't answer to any of us.''

There was a tense air between her and the manager. Zara searched in her bag for her phone, taking it to a quieter place. His phone was on, she hoped with each ring he would answer. Her heart skipped a beat when he did.

"Where are you?'' she whispered into the phone. "Ted isn't happy.''

"I'll be there in two minutes. I needed to deal with something,'' he sounded hassled.

"Yeah, you need to be on the sodding bus, unless you're walking to Stamford Bridge. What are you playing at? Hurry up because I won't have Ted screaming at me.'' She hung up and stomped back to Ted. He was outside pacing by the team coach.

"He will be here in two minutes. He wouldn't tell me what he was doing and, in all honesty, I don't want to know.'' There wasn't time for a debate as Jake came running around the corner, looking bedraggled, but at least he was here.

"Thanks,'' Ted said. As Zara walked away, the bellow from the manager made her jump.

"Where the fuck have you been, Maddox?!''

"Gaffer, I'm sorry, I'll…''

"Get on the coach, I don't have time to hear it now. That's two week's wages docked.'' Jake was smart enough at this point to not argue.

The coach pulled away, finally headed to the match. Zara made her way back to help Jenny. They would head back to Valcoast after the match. Before she entered the hotel, she noticed a man out of the corner of her eye. He was leaning against the wall, watching her. Black cap, sunglasses, and his leather jacket collar up to cover his face.

"I hope your boyfriend does as he's told today. If not, I'll be seeing you again,'' he said, his voice low and threatening. It was the same man from outside her flat.

"What is your problem?'' Zara snapped. ''Leave me alone.'' Black cap man sniggered, "I will if the score is acceptable.''

Zara felt her blood run cold. What did the score have to do with anything?

"Are you obsessed with Jake or something, or is it me? You can get arrested for stalking.''

It happened so quickly, Zara had no time to react. He grabbed her wrist and pulled her down the side of the hotel. His hand clenched her throat as he pushed her against the wall.

"I've tried being nice, but you are not getting it. A lot is riding on Valcoast going down this season.''

Her heart dropped into her stomach.

"No,'' she gasped, the pressure on her throat tightening. It all fell into place. Jake's sudden drop in form almost overnight. The mixed signals and drinking before a game.

"Now I have your full attention. Loverboy is their talisman. My boss needed him to make his plan work. He wouldn't play nicely, so we made it difficult for him to refuse.''

"What did you do?'' Zara hissed. Another snigger, and a forceful push further against the wall.

"Every time he thinks we won't retaliate, we make sure he knows we will. Poor Rosie Boxall, though, she's on the mend. No harm done. If Jake hadn't got cocky that morning, it wouldn't have happened. He doesn't say no to us."

"No!' Zara screamed. "She's a baby.''

"Now Jake knows, if he cares about his teammates and you, he will do as he is told. On or off the pitch, we own him.''

"He wasn't playing, therefore he couldn't ensure he controlled the game. Red cards don't let him off the hook.''

Zara tried to fight back. He was stronger, and he held her firm.

"For all our sakes, we need to do our jobs.''

"I want to know why? What's so important about a club going down?'' Zara struggled to speak.

"Money. If we relegate them this season, my boss gets the club for less. Blake wants to sell and he has a deal already set up. Trouble is, my boss is a very rich man, but selfish with his money. He gets the club for less if we relegate them. Then Jake can rise from the ashes, be the hero again, and take them back up. We all need to be smart.''

"What?!'' Zara was stunned. ''He can't do that!'' Zara hissed. ''You're destroying him''

"How sweet. Is he finding things hard? Are you helping him through it? I bet you make him feel better at night?'' He sneered, his breath smelling of cigarettes. His evil eyes moved down, looking at her with a leer that what unsettling.

"You'd make me feel better, I'll give him credit, he gets the good-looking ones,'' he pulled a phone from his pocket and angled it showing his hand around her throat. "Just in case he needs more incentive.''

"Don't send it, please," Zara cried out. She heard the sound of the message sending. "You're disgusting."

"Don't be a hero, Miss Rose. Jake already tried that. I wouldn't want to pay a visit to your new friend too."

Zara shook her head, "What?"

"She's a lovely woman...that Mrs. Virgo. Cute kids, too. Now you and Jake are a team, make sure he does as he's told," he released her and stalked off, disappearing as quickly as he appeared. Leaving her paralysed to the spot, watching the space where her attacker once stood. The pieces all clicked together, a puzzle now complete. Zara used the side of the hotel to steady herself.

"Oh, Jake," She whispered to herself. No wonder he was all over the place. He wasn't losing his skills, he was hiding them. The image of Jamie running from the stadium after they almost killed his daughter and the guilt Jake must have felt over that was overwhelming her.

If she wasn't sure about helping Jake before, she was now. Her mind raced with the possible outcomes and all of them were bad for everyone. Jake would lose the most, and it wasn't fair. For the moment, Zara had to stay calm, think things through, and talk to Jake. He didn't have to fight this alone any longer. There must be a way, but none without severe consequences for Jake and the club. Throwing games wasn't just frowned upon, it was a criminal offence. Being under duress must hold some favour. Surely, for protecting his teammates and their families and herself. Bile rose in her throat and anger ripped through her. This was her club, and these were her friends. Jake was something more than a friend, and she wouldn't let this happen. For now, she had to continue as normal. Taking a few minutes to compose herself, she settled her nerves and returned to Jenny.

"Where have you been?'' Jenny asked while piling plates into a large dishwasher. ''I thought you'd headed to Stamford Bridge with the team.'' Her laugh echoed around the kitchen, "Did Jake make the coach?''

Zara nodded.

"Oh, thank god.''

"I'm not feeling too good. I just needed a minute,'' Zara lied, guilt consumed her. Jenny went into mother mode forcing Zara to sit down.

"I'm ok, honestly. I had a dizzy spell, but it's passed now.''

"Have you eaten enough? You've been on the go since six. I get that way if I don't eat properly.''

Zara pretended to think about the question. "Actually, I haven't eaten. I forgot breakfast," Zara replied lying. Jenny tutted, shaking her head.

"Silly girl. I have some eggs left. I'll make you a roll. We have time to rest now."

The thought of eating churned Zara's stomach, but if it kept her boss from asking more questions, she would force it down.

"Where did Jake go?" Jenny asked, a mouth full of an egg roll. "I worry about him." The egg tasted sour in Zara's mouth. Keeping a poker face, she nodded in agreement.

"Has he said anything to you?" Jenny asked. This was the last thing Zara wanted to talk about.

"No, he gets defensive if I bring it up." It was close to the truth.

"What is the deal with you two?" Jenny wiped her face with a napkin, looking intently at Zara.

"I don't know. One minute he's all friendly and the next he's acting all offish. I suppose at this moment we are just friends, nothing has happened between us. Not like that, anyway."

"Do you want it to be more?" her boss asked.

Zara shrugged, "Sometimes…maybe. Then when he acts like a jerk, no.''

Jenny laughed, "Typical man. I'm sure he will sort himself out. He's having a bad patch and when players hit a wall in their careers, they sulk about it. Ted will get him back on track.''

If only it was that simple. Zara couldn't wait for this game to be over. The dread that filled her as kick-off approached was unbearable. How was Jake, what was going through his mind? Should she text him and let him know she was okay, and that he had her on his side, or would that put more pressure on him. She decided it was best said in person.

Three o'clock approached, and the players made their way out. The roar of the crowd was deafening. They watched from the hotel. Jenny kitted out in her shirt, a scarf around her neck. Her red hair hung loose, it made her look younger. Her excitement was already at its peak.

"Come on, boys!'' she yelled at the television. Zara was the only person who could see the torment in Jake's eyes. To others he looked focused, thinking about the game. He was, but not in the way others thought. If he played badly, it was more points dropped. If he played well, who knows who was next on the list.

As the referee blew the whistle to start the game, Zara watched intently at Jake's every move. The pass that he should have picked up, the run he would have taken earlier a few weeks ago, it was all deliberate. The shot at goal just aimed slightly off target. Jake Maddox could score goals with his eyes shut. It must kill him to pretend to be so bad, to go against his instinct. It was hurting her to watch him suffer.

The camera scanned the crowd, and there was her mystery man in the crowd watching his every move. Then they showed the families cheering them on. Rosie Boxall sat on her mother's knee, her arm in a cast. The bruising to her face. That little girl was a cruel reminder of just how ruthless and evil these people were. Zara would risk herself, but not a child. Fighting back the tears, she attempted to watch the game with Jenny. Twenty minutes into the game, Jamie Boxall fired the ball down the right wing towards Jake, who flicked it to Billy Fox. Billy volleyed it into the back of the net.

"Yes, boys!" Jenny screamed, jumping up and hugging Zara, too elated to notice the lack of celebration. Zara forced herself to mask her fear. Jake had assisted with that goal and he mirrored Zara, forcing the smile and the celebration. At half time Jake got a message to her.

"Are you ok? Please answer this?"

Zara quickly replied.

"Yes, I'm with Jenny at the hotel. I know everything. I need to see you later. We need to talk, but I'm on your side. I know it isn't your fault. Who are these people?"

Jake tapped back.

"I don't know what to do. I want to kill him."

Zara had a thought. It wasn't ideal.

"You have to get off that pitch, somehow."

There was no response to that, and she waited for the game to restart. As the minutes ticked by, Jake looked sluggish, and at the sixty-eighth minute, he collapsed to the floor. He lay motionless and the medical staff ran to his aid. Jenny was in tears as she watched. Zara had her hands to her face, knowing he was putting on an act but hoping this worked.

"Oh no, they are getting the stretcher." Jenny gasped. "What happened?"

"Nobody was near him. He just collapsed!" Zara replied. Jenny looked at her.

"He will be ok," Jenny assured her, patting her arm in comfort. This woman was the sweetest person, and Zara hated the fact she was fooling her. All she had to do was wait until they were home and she could finally talk to him, face to face. But waiting was too much, Zara ran from the hotel. Her legs powered her forward and she didn't stop until she reached Stamford Bridge. The game must be almost over. And then she heard the roar. It was too loud to be a goal for Valcoast. That was the Chelsea fans celebrating.

A draw, would that be less of an impact?

Jake assisted a goal and only a point. Some hope for the team and the fans. Fewer points to keep people safe. It was the best outcome for now. The final whistle sounded and fans piled out, a sea of blue shirts and smiling Chelsea fans surrounded her. Then she saw him, his eyes on her, stalking forward with a purpose. She was alone in this, and she couldn't scream for help because her next move could expose Jake. Zara ran back towards the hotel and seemed to lose him. When she stopped to take a breath, knowing she was close to safety, he appeared again, this time in front of her.

"Zara, what did I say..."

"Stay the fuck away from me. I'll tell everyone what you've done," she threatened. He laughed cruelly.

"I wouldn't be so stupid. Do you think Jake would ever recover from this? His career would be over. They would crucify him. He will never play again. He will have to answer to his club, his teammates, the FA, the press, and the fans. So, before you open that pretty mouth of yours, think about the backlash it would cause.''

 He pulled a piece of paper from his pocket and handed it to her, "Open it. It's a little incentive.'' He crossed the road and headed out of sight. Her hands shaking, she unfolded the paper, "Oh No!''

It was Jenna Virgo taking her kids to school. They already had their next target. Pulling her phone from her back pocket, she called Jenna.

"Zara, I'm so pleased to hear from you. Is Jake ok?''

"I don't know. I'm worried. I'm sorry to call, but didn't know who else I could.''

Jake's collapse was a perfect excuse, "I'm waiting to hear. How are you and the boys?''

"I'm sure he's being looked after. Let me know as soon as you hear anything. The boys are all good, running riot at my brother's house.''

"You are not at the game?'' Zara held back from cheering.

"No, it's my brother's birthday. He's having a family gathering, so we watched it all together.''

The panic levelled out and Zara pretended she was calm.

"At least it was a draw,'' Jenna said, with a sigh of relief. "Great pass by Jake, I knew he wouldn't let a bad patch keep him down for long.'' Jenna chatted like they were old friends. "He'll be ok?''

"I hope so.''

"Zara, he's as strong as an ox, I'm sure he's fine. You weren't out partying last night, were you?'' Jenna joked. ''Sorry too soon,'' she quickly said.

"Not last night, this was absolutely nothing to do with me,'' Zara bantered back. ''I don't think dinner will happen tonight, can we postpone? Let's see how Jake is later.'' Dinner with Jenna and Ben was not on her priorities, even if she wished it was her only plan.

"Fair enough. I'm sure Ben will call soon, I'll text you. I know you say you two are not a thing, but you care about him, that's obvious. I'll keep you updated.''

"Thanks, Jenna. He isn't a bad person,'' the words had left her mouth without thinking about it. Her loyalty was already strong.

"I know, Zara. I have known Jake for a long time. He's a good guy, despite what the press likes to say. Who said he isn't?'' Jenna had not let her words go unnoticed.

Zara thought fast, "Nobody, just all the negativity about him lately is getting to me.''

"Blimey, you've known him a few weeks and the WAG in you is strong.'' Jenna cackled. Zara hated the title of WAG. It made her cringe.

"I'm no WAG, I'm just the kitchen girl,'' Zara said bitterness in her tone.

"Don't say that!'' Jenna snapped. "You're lovely, don't let anyone tell you otherwise. With Jake or not, we are friends.''

That made Zara smile, but the guilt of her secret turned it quickly into a frown. After hanging up, she trudged back to the hotel. Jenny was pacing outside and looked pleased to see Zara heading back.

"Any news?'' Jenny called before she'd got near her. Shaking her head, Zara explained the game was over before she'd got there.

"Let's get home,'' Jenny said, linking her arm and leading her back inside. "Things will be ok. I promise.''

Zara knew nothing would be okay.

9

Zara watched the day's sports news back at her flat. Jake's collapse dominated it. Speculations being thrown around as people waited for a statement from the club. A wave of slight anger towards Jake, she'd expected to hear something from him. Her messages went unanswered. Jenna knew nothing, at least that was what she told Zara. He was being assessed by medical staff, which was all Ben had told his wife.

A terrible thought crept into Zara's mind. Had something really happened, or was it fake? Had his tormentors taught him a lesson? She paced her living room, feeling lost. Her dad was calling again, she couldn't continue to avoid his calls. A friendly voice might help while she waited.

"Hi, Dad."

"You're alive then?" it relieved him to hear her voice, but with an undertone of annoyance.

"Why have you been ignoring our calls?"

"I'm sorry, this has been intense. I'm fine, don't worry." A brief pause before her dad spoke.

"Are you going to tell us what the bloody hell is going on?" he was angry. "I see my daughter splashed all over the news, and you won't tell us what is true or not."

Zara curled up on the sofa and told her dad as much as she could. He listened without interrupting her. When she had told him the things he could know, she waited for his reaction.

"Shit!" was his first response. "Are you dating Jake Maddox?"

"No. Yes. Maybe. I don't know." Her answer could not have been more vague.

"Either you are or you're not."

"We are just friends. Do I like him? Yes. Does he like me? I think so. He's got a lot going on and I'm being a friend to him." She knew she had to trust her dad, give him something honest. He said nothing at first. He was processing her words.

"His poor form, you're helping him?"

"Something like that Dad. He's a good guy, and he needs good people around him. I don't know if he's ok, and I am worried.''

"He couldn't get any better than you, darling. I'm glad he has you. Is he nice to you?''

"Yes, Dad, he is. He's just a normal guy that's having a rough patch.''

He gave the usual dad talk to be careful, and if he hurt her, he would hunt him down.

"If you need anything, your mother and I are right behind you. The press are shit bags. When you know more, please let us know. We won't repeat anything you tell us. I promise you that.''

They chatted longer, and she felt better after putting her dad at ease. Her mother spoke for a few minutes and she could hear the concern in her voice, but she assured them that she was fine. Then she called Rachel. It upset her, being ignored. It was understandable. Rachel had thought she was moving on with her new famous friends.

"Don't be silly! Rach, you are always my number one. I'm sorry. It's just been a crazy week. I love you more than anyone. Nobody will ever take your placc.'' Rachel took more convincing than her dad, but eventually, she let it go.

"All I have seen is gossip spreading. I want to smash all their nasty heads in. You not answering my calls hurt.''

"I know. I didn't mean to. I was just getting my head around it all. I didn't want to drag anyone else into it.''

"I'm your best friend. We stand together,'' Rachel said, her voice fearless at defending her oldest friend. "They take you on, they take me on too. That's how it will always be.'' It made Zara laugh.

"Am I forgiven?'' Rachel left her hanging for a few seconds. "Yeah, don't do it again. How is Jake?'' Zara told her the same as she'd told her dad.

"I'm sure he will be fine. If you need me, call, ok?'' Rachel comforted Zara.

Zara felt better once she'd hung up. Having people she fully trusted on her side made it easier to cope. Talking helped, even if she couldn't tell them the full truth. Knowing you had people who cared about you was better than the feeling of being alone.

She tried Jake again, still nothing. An hour passed, and she was just drifting off to sleep on the sofa when a knock on her front door woke her up. At first, she was reluctant to answer it, not expecting anyone. What if it was him, the mystery man? Another loud knock. Checking her peephole, she quickly opened the door.

"Jake!'' He was in a tracksuit, and his hood up, shielding his face. She pulled him inside, shutting the door to block the world out. He stood awkwardly looking at her.

"What happened?'' She asked.

"I faked passing out. They've spent hours checking me over. Obviously, there is nothing wrong with me. I said I felt dizzy and fainted. Hopefully, they will just put it down to a random incident. I've been told to rest and skip training tomorrow. Brian drove me here. Gaffer knows I'm not right. The man isn't stupid.'' His phone rang and after checking who was calling, his expression showed disdain.

''Fuck sake.'' He hissed.

Zara took his phone. He didn't stop her. It was Ivy.

"She has been calling since the match. Pretending to care.''

Zara answered the call. It was time to make it clear to Ivy, Jake was no longer her business.

 "What?!'' Zara snapped.

"Err.. who is this?'' Ivy's irritating voice shrilled down the phone.

"Jake isn't available. Stop calling,'' Zara demanded.

Silence.

"I just want to know he's alright?' Who is this?''
her voice getting more high-pitched.

"I'm a friend. Jake is no longer your concern. Leave
him alone.''

"Are you that slapper? Kara, or whatever.'' Ivy
snapped.

"It's Zara. And I think you need to read up on the
term Slapper. You fit more into the category than I
do.''

Jake's eyes went wide, awe on his face. Seeing
someone stand up to his ex was satisfying. Ivy had
dominated her way into everything over the years,
used her fierce attitude to control many people. Jake
wasn't the first footballer she'd snared over the
years.

"You cheeky little bitch! Put Jake on the phone.''

"Are you stupid too? He doesn't want to talk to you.
Now, back the fuck off!'' rage engulfed her. The
self-absorbed bint wouldn't bully her. What people
didn't know about Zara was she was no pushover.
You treat her with respect and you got it back. Her
dad had always taught her to be strong. Let no one
walk all over you. It was that moment she knew this
thing with Jake had to stop, she just needed to make
that happen.

"We don't have time for this, Ivy. Have a pleasant life.'' she cut the call, and Zara forgot about Ivy Mason.

"I think that's her being told,'' Jake commented, holding back a snigger. ''Ivy isn't used to being ignored.''

"Sounds like that's her problem,'' Zara replied. ''We have more important things to worry about.'' Jake smiled despite his troubles.

"Why did you come here?'' Zara asked, leading him to her kitchen. He sat at her small dining table. She felt a sudden bit of embarrassment. Her small flat was nothing compared to his beautiful house, although he seemed not to notice. ''Sorry about the mess.'' Her cheeks felt flushed. Jake looked around him.

"What mess? It's a nice place,'' he was being polite, she told herself. "I just wanted to see you,'' he didn't look at her. "I'm sorry you're caught up in this mess.''

Zara took the seat next to him. Turning to face him, she took his hands in hers. "Tell me everything, from the start.''

He held onto her hands like they were his lifeline.

"Did he hurt you?'' he asked first, checking her neck. Zara assured him she was fine.

"It started a few weeks ago. Everything was great, and I didn't have a care in the world. Apart from Ivy. That was my only issue. I'd been unhappy for months. She was overbearing. I was like her possession and she spent money, my fucking money I might add, every day. Not that I'm a tight bastard, but she just assumed it was hers. I was on my way to end it with her. I was leaving training. And then our new 'friend' approached me. I thought he was a fan at first. He said I needed to do as they asked me, I thought he was mucking about, only he wasn't. People would get hurt if I didn't start ensuring we lost.'' Jake put his head in his hands. "I told him to fuck off. I'm a winner. I don't lose.''

Jake had point-blank refused and walked to his car. Once he arrived home, he thought it might have been a prank or a chancer. He tried to forget it had happened. The next morning, a letter was posted through his letterbox. A picture of his mum outside her house.

"If you love your mother, don't be an idiot." It made Jake take notice. More pictures came through teammates, their families, Jenny, anyone who he was close to. Even Ivy. And although she was irritating, he wouldn't see her hurt. They'd been happy once, albeit for a short time. He couldn't risk it.

"I'm scared,'' he said once he'd told her everything.

"I'm scared too, but we have to stop this. But we need help,'' Jake shook his head, panic in his eyes.

"No. I can't tell anyone. Do you understand what will happen to me? I will lose everything.'' He stood, letting go of her hands.

''I can't cope with this,'' he was shaking as he paced around her kitchen. ''I need to go. I need to stay away from you.'' He headed to her front door.

"Jake!'' Zara followed. "I'm already involved. It isn't just about us. They are ruthless, they are evil. Rosie Boxall wasn't an accident.''

Jake froze, his back to her. ''What?!'' he hissed. Zara pulled him back to her.

"Our 'friend' told me it was him that ran down Rosie,'' Jake's legs buckled beneath him. Zara caught him and he gripped her.

"I don't think it matters anymore, you staying away from me. They've connected us regardless,'' Jake looked down at her as she spoke. ''I need you as much as you need me.''

At first, he didn't respond, then his head leaned down and she felt his lips press against hers. He pulled her against him as the kiss intensified. She felt his toned body mould into hers, his grip on her tightened, holding her against him.

"I've wanted this since the first day I saw you," he whispered breathlessly.

"What took so long?" Zara replied. He pulled away looking her in the eye.

"You know why…"

"Because I'm the kitchen girl."

Jake stepped back, anger on his face. "You think I'm that shallow?" his eyes narrowed.

Zara had meant it as a joke, but that had backfired. "No. It was a joke. But I'm no model."

"So!" Jake snapped. "You are beautiful. It took me so long because it scared me you'd get hurt."

He pulled her back to him, kissing her again. It was obvious where this was leading and as much as she wanted him, she had to resist. It took all of Zara's strength to stop it.

"What's wrong?" Jake asked, looking concerned. "Don't you like me?"

"Yes, I just want things to go slower. I know that's weird, and there are thousands of women who wouldn't hesitate, but…" Jake put a finger to her lips, silencing her.

"You want to wait?"

Zara nodded. "I want to get to know you, not Jake the footballer, just Jake."

His smile was a relief, he seemed happy with it too. "OK."

"You don't mind?" Zara asked needing reassurance.

"Whatever you want. I'm not a jerk. I won't force you to do anything you don't want to." Zara kissed him again. A lingering kiss that sparked things again. "You know, you are making it difficult to hold back.,' he chuckled as her cheeks flushed.

"Sorry," she said, stepping away and grabbing a bottle of wine from the fridge. "No training tomorrow?" Zara said, waving the bottle in the air.

His phone vibrated, "Bollocks."

He complained as he pulled away. Zara stepped back. His kiss still lingered on her lips. It was Jake's agent.

"I'm fine. They've checked me over. I don't know what happened," he said, trying to sound convincing.

Zara let him talk in private. His agent was one of the best. He was in expert hands with Barry

Greyson. She waited in her small living room, staying away from his personal calls. When he joined her, he took the space next to her on her sofa, put his head on her shoulder. Zara rested her head on his.

"What do we do now?" he asked.

"If I knew that answer, Jake, I'd be doing it. I know it scares you to tell anyone, but I don't know if we can get out of this alone."

He sighed and closed his eyes. The stress was showing. He wasn't sleeping or eating as he should.

"I'm going to lose everything," his eyes were open again, looking up at her. His hair was dirty, she noticed. It smelled of mud and sweat. He was still breath-taking despite it. She fought against the need to rip his clothes off.

"I don't know what I will do without football. It's all I know…all I have ever wanted. I'd rather die than be something else," he said breaking her X-rated thoughts.

"Don't say that!" Zara snapped. It crushed her, hearing him say those words. But she knew he meant it. If he lost his career, she knew he would do something stupid. Go off the rails. Zara knew those words had cemented in her mind what she felt for him. She was in love with him. She should run from this mess, but she couldn't, and she wouldn't. If she could keep him here, lock him away, she would. Jake Maddox couldn't hide, he had too much at stake.

"Losing my career is one thing, but losing it in a cloud of shame. I can't even process the thought. I love the game, the club, it's my home. They are my family and I am killing it all. I'm taking everyone down with me. Why me?!''

Zara smiled at him, ''You won't lose anything. I don't know how to fix it, but we will.''

He reached up and stroked her cheek.

"I love your fierceness, but I don't think this will end well. Don't fight for me, it's not worth your life. I care too much for you to put you at risk.''

Zara stood up and paced the room.

"I think that's my choice to make. Our 'friend' said we are a team. That I should make sure you do what they need. What he didn't bank on was who he teamed you up with. They bullied me in school, my ex bullied me, and I'm still standing. I beat them, and I'll beat these bastards.''

She's always drew strength when challenged. Every time someone tried to break her, she rose above it. Rachel had become her best friend after stepping in at school. She'd seen her bullied and one day decided enough was enough. It had been Rachel who'd spoken to Zara's dad about her concerns with her last relationship. She knew something was wrong, and it was her that had pulled her back to her senses.

Jake sat up straight, "Bullied by your ex?''

It had been a few months since she'd removed the shackles of a controlling relationship. A painful memory, but she trusted Jake to tell him everything. He listened to her, silent as she relived the controlling behaviour. She spoke of the isolation. It was slow at first from her family and friends. She was lucky that people had picked up on things and didn't allow things to spiral. There was never any violence, but he used mental abuse to dent her confidence.

"It's hard to forget when someone makes you fear your own decisions or tells you not to eat because you are getting fat.''

"What?!'' Jake spat. "He stopped you from eating?'' Zara nodded.

"The fucking prick!'' Jake was enraged. "I'll kill him and the other prick from earlier. Seeing that picture…'' He shook his head.

"No, you won't. He's not worth it,'' she stated. She felt nothing for him anymore. "He said I would be alone if I left him. That I wasn't loveable and I should be grateful to him… How wrong was he?'' she smiled at Jake.

"He was very wrong,'' Jake smiled back. "Come here.''

He took her hand, pulled her back to him. "He was an idiot to let you go. You're perfect. His loss.'' He kissed her again until she pulled away.

Pouring the wine and settling next to him, she felt completely at home with him.

"You can stay here if you want to.''

"I thought you'd never ask,'' he laughed.

"Tell me how you got into professional football,'' Zara asked, interested to know his story, in his own words. She sipped her wine, leaning into the curl of his body, his arm wrapped around her shoulders.

"What do you want to know?'' he asked.

"Everything. Where did you play as a kid? What are your parents like?''

Jake took a long sip of wine and told her about his passion for the game had started as young as three years of age. He was always kicking a ball, had played in an under 5s team, and moved up with age. He played all the time: at school, in the garden, in the street, and in the living room.

"The number of things I've broken over the years is numerous," Jake laughed remembering. "Pictures, vases, and a couple of windows to name a few. As for my parents, they are legends. They always made sure me and Darren had everything we needed. Darren is my younger brother. He's still at school and in his last year. He'll be sixteen next month, but he'll always be a little shit, no matter how old he gets.'' Jake joked before his smile dropped.

"What?'' Zara asked, picking up his mood change.

"Darren has always looked up to me. I wonder how can he be proud of me now. He's doing so well with his football, he wants to be just like me.'' He sighed for a moment and then came back to it. He continued talking fondly of his family. His mum worked two jobs, for his dad to work but always be on hand to drive Jake wherever he needed to be.

"They sacrificed a lot for my career. When I joined Valcoast's youth Academy at thirteen, it was the first time I saw my Dad cry. He was so proud. Now, I'm pissing all over their efforts.''

This was what Zara wanted to know about Jake. This was the real him: passionate, hard-working, driven, and caring. He saw her expression.

"Don't tell anyone I said all that. I've got a hard man reputation to uphold,'' Jake joked.

"You're a big softy, aren't you?'' Zara whispered. He responded with another kiss.

"Not on the pitch, I'm not. I fought for my place and lost a good friend over it,'' he said this with regret.

"I think I know about this. Stevie Howes?'' Zara said, knowing some of this from old news articles. Jake had known him since school and had come through the youth academy with him. He'd done nothing wrong apart from being a better player. Stevie had begrudged him for it.

 "Things seemed ok. He was going to Fulham, but injury ended his career early. It had damaged his left knee. It healed enough so he could walk, but not to play football. Medical doctors said it was too weak.''

"That's not your fault. You shouldn't feel bad about that. Why did you fall out?''

Jake looked embarrassed, "I'm not proud of it. I swear I didn't know they were serious.''

Zara's eyebrows arched, "Oh Jake, don't tell me you stole his girl?''

"No, not really stole, but might have had a stupid drunken one-night stand. I swear I had no idea he was in love with her. I thought it was just…'' he stopped. Zara had a disapproving look on her face. '

"You're right. I've no excuse. I was eighteen and an idiot. I think it was just the last straw. He couldn't compete with me. I didn't set out to do it. I wanted a place in the team, and I got it fair and square. The girl, that was wrong, but they had only known each other a week. I regret losing him as a friend. I've tried to reach out to him, but he doesn't want to know. It's been seven years since we spoke.'' He seemed embarrassed by his admission. "Have I blown it?''

Zara laughed.

"We all do stupid things. I'm not perfect either. I stole a Twix from a shop when I was eleven,'' Jake reeled back from her, shock on his face.

"You're a chocolate bar thief! That's disgraceful!''

They laughed until they remembered the dark cloud hanging over them. Jake looked exhausted.

"Let me cook," Zara said, leaving the comfort of Jake's arm. "You need to eat. Maybe a good meal will help us think of a plan.''

"Sounds great. I'm starving.''

An hour later they tucked into spaghetti Bolognaise and homemade garlic bread. Jake piled the grated cheese on top.

"It's the best bit.''

He didn't speak while he ate.

"This is so good,'' he remarked halfway through before tucking back in. It felt so natural, them having dinner like a normal couple. Was that what they were?

"So, what do we do now? Do we act like friends or...'' Zara braved the question.

Jake stopped eating and looked her in the eyes. "That's up to you?''

Me?''

"Yeah. If we go public, it will turn into a fucking circus. If you want to be...'' he paused, unsure of himself. "I mean, I would like you to be my girlfriend if that's what you want.''

Zara hadn't expected that response. Deep down, she'd prepared herself for rejection. "Oh,'' she felt herself getting flushed. "Err... Me?''

"I don't see anyone else here.''

Zara knew her life would truly change if she said yes.

"...or have I misread this?''

Zara shook her head and grabbed his hand. "It's already a circus. It might as well be worthwhile. You still owe me a hat-trick.''

Jake smiled, "I owe you much more than that." He winked and shoved more spaghetti in his mouth. Zara pondered on how it would go down with the world and quickly decided she didn't care. Her phone sat next to her plate, and she picked it up.

"Might as well rip off the plaster,'' a defiant smile on her face. Aiming the camera at Jake, who automatically knew how to position himself, she took a few and he posed confidently. He had become immune to his picture being taken.

"Here we go.'' She said. She uploaded one picture with the caption:

Taking care of this one. Nothing keeps him down.

She tagged him and it only took seconds before her phone went nuts. She didn't bother looking, but she warned her family and friends. The rest of the evening flew by. He stayed in her bed and kept his promise of taking it slow. But it was nice to fall asleep in his arms and have someone to kiss goodnight. Keep them keen, isn't that how the saying goes?

10

Jenny waved Zara over. She was excited about something.

"I stayed up all night getting this ready. Do you think she will like it?" On the counter stood a beautiful pink cake. The theme was fairies. "Kirsty is bringing Rosie in today, she's doing better."

The lump in Zara's throat nearly choked her. "Oh, Jen, it's beautiful. She will love it."

"Really?" Jenny had been so upset over the accident and couldn't wait to hug the little girl.

"Rosie has been begging to come in and see everyone. She loves it here. Can you help me set up a corner of the restaurant? Make her a VIP."

How could she refuse, but the sense of guilt was overwhelming? It was a way to make things better. Rosie was safe and alive.

"Hopefully, they will lock the sick bastard up," Jenny said, her voice filled with anger.

"Sorry?"

"Haven't you heard? They think they have the driver." This caught Zara's attention.

"What!" Zara nodded. "When, who?"

"I don't know details yet. Jamie was with the police this morning. That's why he was late for training." Handing a large carrier bag to Zara, Jenny relayed the message she'd had from her friend on the Physio team. "Last night someone called in with some information. They have arrested someone. If it is the culprit, I hope he has a good fucking lawyer. Jamie will destroy him."

"That's great!" Zara said. Did it mean their stalker was off the street? Could it mean this was over? She couldn't help but hope. Rosie would get justice and Jake could be free too. She got to work on Rosie's VIP table. Pink ribbons covered her seat. Fairies decorated the table with confetti and her cake. Her own special table. It was warming how this small gesture made things seem brighter.

"How are things with you?'' Jenny asked once they'd completed their task. "You know, with Jake?'' Zara blushed.

"It's great. Still early days.'' It was half true. The two of them as a couple were great, but with a dark secret hanging over them it was hard to enjoy it fully.

"I knew you two would get it together. He couldn't take his eyes off you.'' Jenny giggled. "He smiles more lately. If you can get him scoring again, you'll be a hero around here.''

A hero was a far-fetched idea. Zara held her smile and fussed with the decorations on the table, avoiding eye contact. Jake was putting on a brave face around the club. He was saying all the right things, he was trying to focus and get his head back in the game. After several more medical checks, they had confirmed him as fully fit. It had baffled the medical staff and they would watch his fitness like hawks. He couldn't pull that act again. It would cause suspicion. She still hadn't worked out how to get them out of this. There was only a few games left of the season. Time was running out.

The phone rang in the kitchen. Jenny grabbed it gracefully while carrying trays of sandwiches. There was a big meeting scheduled in the main boardroom. That meant it was important. The important conversations went on there. Nobody entered that room unless invited. They set catering up before anyone arrived, to avoid anything leaking out. Although, it didn't take a genius to know it would be about the shocking season.

"Shit,'' Jenny said, replacing the handset. ''We need more food prepared. Bollocks, like we haven't got enough to do.''

"Why?''

"The big man is arriving,'' Jenny didn't miss Zara's confused look. ''Blake Treviño. This meeting must be bloody important if he's flown over from the states.'' That was when Zara felt the penny drop in her head. He was over to discuss selling the club. It was the most obvious reason.

"Get a few more trays made up, he's bringing his entourage by the sounds of it,'' she rolled her eyes and glided out of the kitchen.

Keith was busy preparing lunch for the players.

"Give me ten minutes and I'll help you,'' Zara promised. Keith nodded and winked. He was good under pressure, never let it get to him.

Once she'd placed the extra trays in the large boardroom, an oval table with leather chairs sat waiting for its visitors. Zara wished she could hear what they would say, to know what the truth was. If anything said in this room could help them. Victor arrived first, just as she was leaving.

"Zara, are we all set?'' he asked looking ready for business, dressed in an expensive suit, not a hair out of place. He looked younger than fifty-six but rumour had it, he wore a wig to hide his bald patch. Also, to make himself look younger.

"Yes, all yours.''

"Thank you. Looks great. I'm starving,'' he smiled as he grabbed a ham sandwich. "We will be here for a few hours, so can you come at two, and check if we need anything else?'' Zara nodded. Maybe this could give her a way in, get something from this. Victor didn't know his request was more welcome than he imagined.

As she headed back to the restaurant, the chatter was loud. Training had finished for lunch. She felt bad she'd not got back in time to help Keith.

"Come on!'' he shouted as she arrived. She quickly took over the counter. The banter quickly began. The players always made her laugh.

"What you doing to Maddox? He's fucking smiling for a change,'' Billy commented as he took his food. "Can I get some too?''

"Oi, keep your hands off her Foxy,'' Jake stalked into the room, eyes on Billy like a sniper.

"How about you score again, Mads? On the fucking pitch, I mean.

"Fuck off. Still scored more than you, on and off the pitch!'' Jake retorted. The comment had hurt more than anyone would ever know, but he had to keep the conversation as banter.

"I'll be back, and you'll be back in your box. Bask in the glory, it's only temporary,'' Billy laughed, but it wasn't convincing. Jake grinned as he walked across the room, leaning over the counter to kiss Zara.

"Get a room. Soppy twat.'' Billy heckled, alerting everyone's attention.

Jake gave him the middle finger. He pulled away, winking. He kissed her again before settling down with Ben at a table, not before giving Billy a playful Jab on his way past. His relationship with Billy was interesting. They bantered constantly and you'd question if they even liked each other. It was clear Billy idolized Jake, but he'd never admit it. A football team was all about competition. On the pitch, in the dressing room, training and even sitting around eating. They all wanted to be the best. Ultimately, no matter what, they had each other's backs. Then there was a commotion at the back of the room.

"Rosie!'' Jenny gushed. "Oh, my word!''

The little girl ran into the room, arm still in a cast. Her strawberry blonde hair in bunches, tied with pink ribbons to match her pink Barbie onesie. She clutched a Barbie in her uninjured arm. You wouldn't think two weeks ago this sweet girl was run down by a lunatic. Her bruises were fading, but her smile had not. She ran to Jenny, who picked her up for a tight hug. Jamie and his wife Kirsty stood close together watching their daughter. The players fussed around the small girl; she gave each one a high-five. Jake held back a little. The guilt must be unbearable. Rosie squealed when she saw her VIP table.

"Mummy, Daddy, look!'' Rosie pointed at her table. ''Pretty.'' Jamie scooped his daughter up, placing a kiss on her forehead. He gently placed her on her seat.

"Jenny, this is brilliant,'' pride on his face. "That's so nice of you!'' Kirsty Boxall gushed. Zara noticed tears in her eyes. "You didn't have to do all this.'' Jenny hugged her tightly.

"We wanted to, didn't we, Zara?'' Her boss looked over at her.

"Of course. It was our pleasure.''

Kirsty tilted her head in Zara's direction. "So, you're the famous Zara,'' holding her hand out. Zara shook it.

"Nice to meet you. We are so pleased to see Rosie back here safe.''

"Thanks, it's been a horrible few weeks,'' Kirsty replied, her voice cracking a little. The stress was clear on her face. "We are just thankful she is okay.''

The women chatted more about Rosie. Across the room, Jake watched the small child. She turned, spotting him, and waved across the room.

"Jakey!''

He couldn't ignore her. He forced a smile and crossed the room. She looked up at him. Her expression was thoughtful.

"Why can't you score goals anymore?''

Her mum gasped, "Rosie!'' She looked at Jake. "Sorry.''

"But Mummy, he used to be so good. I just wanted to know if it's because he's sad?'' there was silence in the room. Rosie wasn't saying these things to be mean. There was a genuine concern in her voice. She patted the chair next to her. Jake took the seat with his smile still firmly on his face. Rosie threw her arms around his neck, hugging him.

"When I'm sad, Mummy and Daddy give me hugs to make me happy again. I thought it might help and you can have some of my cake.''

"Thank you, Rosie,'' Jake said, leaning forward and whispering. "Let's hope it works.'' Rosie nodded.

"It'll be okay, you just need to think good things, like cute cats or bunny rabbits.'' Everyone laughed, emotion in everyone's eyes.

"I'll try that,'' Jake promised. She turned her attention to her dad, who was cutting the cake. "I want the biggest bit, Daddy.'' Once everyone had a slice of the bright pink fairy cake, Jamie stood to address the squad.

"We had some news last night. They think they have the scumbag who hit our Rosie.'' A cheer went up around the room.

"He's being investigated, and we should know something soon. All we know so far is a twenty-year-old stole a car and doesn't have a license. If it is him, he better hope they lock him up securely. If I ever get close to him, I'll kill him.''

Jake threw Zara a look. They were both thinking the same thing. Had they had caught their mystery man? Jenny tapped her watch and Zara remembered she had to check on the meeting. It was getting close to two. Leaving the room she let out a breath, Jake and Rosie had been hard to watch and Jamie's revelation had thrown her. Before she reached the door to the meeting room, a hand closed around hers, pulling her into an empty side room.

"Jake, I need to go.''

"I just needed a minute,'' he said kissing her, holding her tight. "That was so shit. It's great seeing Rosie doing well, but what if…'' Zara put her hand over his mouth to silence him.

"Stop. She's doing fine. This isn't your fault. If they have the person responsible, at least Jamie and his family can get closure,'' Jake sighed, nodded, and managed a strained smile. "One day, once this mess is over, you can go out on that pitch and score every goal for her.''

"I will," he nodded with determination.

Zara kissed him quickly before heading to the meeting room. Jake returned to the restaurant. As she approached the door, she heard raised voices. Usually, you couldn't hear the conversations, but disagreements were unfolding. She waited outside the door and certain words made her freeze.

"You are kidding me? No, I don't believe he's past his best. It's a bad patch,'' it was Ted's voice.

"Next transfer window, he's going!''

She knew that voice. It was Blake's. She'd not met him but heard his voice from television and radio interviews.

"Let me work with him," Ted asked again. "He's Valcoast through and through."

"Jake is on borrowed time. I don't have time for waiting. If I don't see improvements in the next few matches, he's done here."

Zara gasped. It was like a hammer came down on her. This was Blake's fault, she thought to herself, selfish bastard does not understand this was all his doing. Taking a few deep breaths, she knocked on the door.

"Come in," Victor responded. The room went silent as she entered.

"Zara, we could do with more teas and coffees," she held her tongue and smiled politely.

"No problem. Anything else?"

"Biscuits. I'm still hungry." Victor said, patting his stomach. Blake nodded, he didn't look at Zara. If she could have lifted one of the metal trays and smashed it over his head, she would have. The vision would have to do. Turning on her heels, she quickly left.

Things had gone from bad to worse.

They were all on borrowed time.

11

Jake was quiet on the drive home later that evening. He hadn't said a word to Zara. His eyes focused on the road ahead.

"Are you going to talk to me?'' Zara finally said, the silent treatment getting on her nerves. She regretted telling Jake about what she'd overheard. It was the wrong thing to do and she worried he might try something stupid.

"I'm sorry, I shouldn't have told you. Please don't be mad with me.''

He removed one hand from the steering wheel, grabbing hers. He lifted it to his lips, kissing it.

"I'm not mad with you. I'm glad you didn't keep it from me. I'm about to lose the club I love…my home. I'm scared," he kissed her hand again. "I should have asked for help when this started. I've dug myself a deeper hole as the weeks go by. If I had gone to Ted, he would have helped me."

"Maybe you still can."

Jake shook his head. "Not after what I've done. I have betrayed everyone," he couldn't see a way out now, but Zara hadn't given up.

"You have been protecting people."

"I did a shit job at that," he was referring to Rosie. "She could have died." He was crying now. The stress had become too much.

"I can't cope with this anymore," his foot pressed on the accelerator. The car increased speed, and his eyes had glazed over.

"Jake!" Zara screamed. "Slow down!"

"Nobody would miss me," he said through gritted teeth.

"Jake, please slow down."

He had zoned out, his mind was somewhere else.

"Jake!" She had never felt scared with him, but she was now. If he didn't stop, they would crash and with the speed hitting over one hundred miles an hour, they would be lucky to survive.

"Fucking stop the car, now!'' her screams were hysterical, and it broke his trance. The look of horror on his face as he realised what he was doing was enough to tell Zara he'd lost control but was back.

"Shit!'' he yelled.

He pressed on the brake, and as they slowed, he pulled the car over. Zara was sobbing.

"I'm sorry…I'm so sorry,'' Jake snapped off his seatbelt, and then hers, and pulled her to him. His arms wrapped around her. "I don't know what came over me.''

Zara was shaking as much as he was. He lifted her head, his hands cradled her face. He kissed her fiercely.

"I'm sorry,'' he repeated it over and over.

"You stupid idiot. You nearly killed us both!'' Zara raged at him. She slapped his face with so much force his head snapped to the side.

"I deserved that,'' he said, rubbing his face.

"Yes, you did," her anger subsided. She knew he needed help and she couldn't do this alone. "Can you drive us home in one piece?"

Jake nodded. "I'll take you home."

"No! I'm not leaving you alone tonight. Take me home with you." Jake didn't argue, he seemed pleased with that.

They drove in silence the rest of the way. In the warmth of his home and a neat whiskey to calm their nerves, the atmosphere was tense between them.

"I'll set up the spare room."

Zara said nothing, and he left the lounge. A few minutes later Zara had calmed. She had thought about the ride home. Jake was under pressure and if they didn't find a solution, she feared what he would do.

"I don't want to stay here," Zara said.

Jake stopped what he was doing, realising he had spoiled everything with his terror ride. He slumped down onto the bed, his head in his hands.

"I'm sorry I lost it. I never meant to scare you. Please don't go…"

Zara knelt in front of him taking his hands from his face. "I mean, I don't want to stay in the spare room."

Jake's eyes went wide, understanding what she meant.

"I'm not leaving you," Zara whispered sweetly. Despite what he had done, her feelings for him hadn't altered. He was under a lot of stress. "Never do that again. Promise me."

He nodded. She grabbed his hand, and they left the half-made spare room. His room was three times bigger, the bed could fit about five people in it. His arms wrapped around her, his muscled frame made her look tiny.

"Who are you Zara Rose?" he kissed her neck. Her eyes closed as she battled with her need for him. She couldn't hold back, not anymore.

She twisted to face him, "I'm all yours. That's who I am."

Jake had never needed someone like he did this girl. This is what others had talked about. When they find that one person and he could never understand the point of it. He could have anyone he wanted. Now, she was all he desired. His dark secret was safe with her. If it had been anyone else, the press would have known about it by now. Ivy loved to leak her whereabouts, meaning their whereabouts at any opportunity. Zara couldn't careless and he liked that. After all, she'd had to deal with because of him, and hadn't run away, spoke volumes about her sincerity. Being without her made him feel sick to his stomach. Seeing that picture of that wankers hands around her throat almost caused him to take it out on every Chelsea player. He didn't because he can't get sent off, that wasn't even a lifeline. His club was growing tired of him and they wanted to get rid of him because he was useless. Nobody would sign him either. He was driftwood and only Zara wanted him. The thoughts spun in his mind like a whirlpool. Her pretty eyes watched him, tears in them.

"You scared me, Jake. It took me back to...'' she stopped. It was then he realised what he'd done. He had been no better than her ex.

"Don't turn out to be like him. I couldn't bear it.''

Jake held her close.

"I promise you, I'm nothing like him. Anything you need to make you trust me, you can have it.''

If she had asked for the most expensive car, diamonds, whatever, he would have had it there the next day. She didn't speak at first, but when she answered, she astonished him once again.

"All I want is you to be back on that pitch and show everybody you haven't given up. I want you to get a fucking hat-trick for me and Rosie. That's all I need.'' Jake stepped backward.

"That's it?'' he wasn't used to answers like that. She bit her lip, a small innocent action that sent his thoughts into overdrive. '*God, she's beautiful'* he thought.

"That's not all I want…'' she glanced at the floor, uncertain to say. "If I have this wrong, don't laugh at me, but wasn't there talk of you being called up for the England squad?''

Jake's eyes lowered and broke his gaze.

"That was before all this started. I've cocked that up.''

That hurt him, undoubtedly it would. Zara pulled him back to her.

"No, you haven't,'' her words were defiant. '''
Don't give up. We will find a way out of this because that's the other thing I want. You, in an England shirt. Because you are fighting for everyone, and nobody knows, and they never will. They think you're arrogant, but they have no fucking idea what you are sacrificing.''

Her words were angry, frustration at the injustice of it all. Knowing if anyone found out they wouldn't see that side, only the scandal of it. "That prick was right about one thing.''

Jake raised his eyebrows, intrigued.

"We are a team and I'm going nowhere. When you need me, I'm ready. I will do what it takes to stop this. If he wants to play dirty, I'm ready with studs up! They created a strike force they don't even see coming..." Jake kissed her to stop her talking. She was undeniably perfect.

She felt his breath on her neck, then the tender brush of lips. His hand knotted in her hair as his kisses became harder and more urgent. Sliding his hand around her waist, he pulled her close to his muscled body. Every desire unravelling for them both.

"Are you sure?" he murmured, pulling away. "You wanted to take it slow?"

Her eyes stared back, inviting him.

"Yes," her hand wound in his blonde hair. "I've waited long enough. I've found my star striker and I'm sealing the deal before the vulture's circle." Her smile was wicked, and he cut off her giggle returning his lips to hers.

12

The kitchen took longer to clean down than normal. It had been a busy Friday. A double training session and three important meetings had kept them all busy. Victor approached with an apologetic look on his face.

"Zara, sorry love. I know you're almost done for the day, but I need some coffees.''

Zara painted on her poker face. Telling him to 'fuck off' wouldn't be sensible.

He held his hands in a prayer sign. "Please. Last-minute meeting. Just coffees.''

Zara sighed but smiled. "Fine. Go sit and I'll bring them over.''

Victor thanked her and took a seat at one of the smaller tables. A few minutes later another man joined him. His face was familiar, but Zara couldn't place him. Taking the coffees over, she caught a few words.

"I think you will be great for our youth team. It's great to see you back here.'' They seemed friendly as she placed the drinks on the table. The visitor looked up at her. He was about the same age as Jake.

"It's Zara, right?'' he asked, his tone warm and friendly. She nodded.

"I'm Stevie. You won't know me, but I know Jake.''

She then realized that she was looking at Stevie Howe.

"It's been a long time since we've spoken though,'' he didn't seem angry as he spoke.

"Stuff from a long time ago, I didn't handle things well.''

Zara took this opportunity to fix something for Jake. "He told me about you, he would love to see you.''

Stevie seemed shocked. "Really? I was a dick the last time he called me.''

"He understands," Zara assured him. "Here's my number, call me later and we can arrange drinks."

Stevie took her number and promised to take her up on the offer. He returned to his meeting with Victor and she headed home.

Jake was playing FIFA on his Xbox when she arrived at his house later that night. Stevie had called her just before she left her flat. She was taking a chance; it was risky. She hoped it was the right thing to do. Sitting next to him as he scored, he turned and kissed her cheek.

"Be nicer if it was an actual goal, during an actual game."

"Jake, I met someone today, and I invited them over," Jake put the controller down and turned to look at her.

"Okay, that's cryptic," his eyes narrowed "Do I get to know who you've invited to my house?"

There wasn't time for her to answer. The doorbell chimed. "I'll get it," Zara said, getting up and skipping to the door.

"Who is it?!" Jake yelled. He was nervous, he didn't like not knowing who was coming to his house. He watched the living room door. A murmured conversation from the hall filtered back to him. Zara appeared again, a smile on her face.

Behind her, Stevie stepped forward into the room.
Jake's bottom jaw nearly hit the floor.

"Stevie," he stood. "What are you doing here?"

His old friend held out his hand, taking a step
forward, his slight limp a reminder of the injury.

"I'm here to clear the air with my best mate."

 Jake was speechless.

"I was in a terrible place a few years ago, and I took
it out on everyone around me. I have been in
counselling for the past twelve months." His hand
remained held out. Jake grabbed it and pulled him
in for a man hug. "Sorry for being such a prick."

"No need, I'm the one who needs to apologise,"
Jake assured him.

Zara left them for a few minutes to grab beers. It
was lovely to see a friendship reforming. Stevie
happily took the beer from Zara. He was already
explaining the past years to Jake. The depression
over losing his career and his anger at everyone in
the world. The girl situation was just another way to
punish Jake for never being as talented as him.

"I hated you for being successful. I didn't care
about the girl, not really. My head was a mess. It
wasn't just about football," he hung his head low
and sighed. "I had a drink and gambling addiction.

Problems I created myself. I gambled away every penny I had.''

This was a shock to hear. Jake put a hand on Stevie's shoulder.

"Shit,'' Jake was processing this information. ''I had no idea. Mate. You could have come to me. I would have helped you.'' Stevie looked ashamed.

"I'll go,'' Zara suggested. They needed time to talk and in private, she didn't need to add to Stevie's embarrassment.

"You don't have to,'' Stevie said, mortified he'd imposed on their evening. ''I'm just glad I've had the chance to clear the air.''

Zara wouldn't stand in the way of them repairing their friendship. "It's okay, you need to talk. I'll see him tomorrow. It was really nice to meet you.''

Stevie smiled at her, ''You too. I'm glad Jake has found a decent woman, for a change.''

Jake walked her to the door.

''Are you sure?'' he checked.

"I think he needs to talk. Sounds like he's been to hell and back, and you both have a lot to talk about,'' Zara kissed him.

"Thank you. I'll take you for dinner tomorrow,'' he promised.

She'd hold him to that.

13

The police cars in the club carpark had caused the media to circle. Zara parked her car and saw Jenny looking distressed while talking to a police officer. As she approached, she saw red marks forming on her boss's face.

"What's happened?"

Jenny burst into tears at seeing Zara, who offered a comforting hug.

"It's awful. I tried to stop them," Jenny explained how she'd arrived earlier than normal. A sleepless night made her get up early. Once inside she heard footsteps, assuming it was the security guard, she shouted good morning.

Jenny was then dragged at knifepoint and forced to open the safe. The man got away with over thirty grand.

Zara held her terrified boss tightly.

"I tried to stop him from taking the money. He said he would…'' Jenny sobbed.

"Sod the money. You're more important.'' Zara assured her.

It wasn't long before everyone arrived at the club. Victor and Blake arrived together. Both coming to Jenny to assure her she had their full support. In the meantime, they gave her orders to go to the hospital to get checked out.

Blake Treviño was sympathetic and saddened by what had happened. As Jenny described her attacker, Zara felt dread in her stomach.

"I didn't see his face, only his eyes. They were evil, Zara. He wore a black cap… it was all such a blur I can't remember. It was too dark,'' Jenny continued to talk but her words faded as Zara knew who had done this. There was only one person it could have been.

"Jenny, get checked out at the hospital. I'll come and pick you up once they've given you the okay.''

A police officer waited to escort her there. After helping her into the police car and assuring her she'd meet her there, Zara headed towards Blake's office. He was sitting at his desk when she arrived. He looked stressed. His skin was ashen.

"Zara, is Jenny ok?'' he asked. She entered and slammed the door.

"Zara?''

"No, she's traumatized. Thank god, she's unhurt. I need to talk to you,'' she blurted out. Blake looked uneasy.

"How can I help?'' he said.

"I heard what you said the other day,'' she spat. Blake sighed and pushed himself away from his desk. ''Yet, you're pretending to give a shit about anyone here.''

He leaned over his desk with a look of indignation.

"Excuse me?'' he slammed his hand down on his desk. "How dare you!''

He was furious, and she cringed, regretting her outburst.

"A well-respected member of this club has been attacked and terrorized, and you come in here making accusations. Get out!'' he was shaking and his fist clenched. "I know you heard what I said about Jake. It is business, and I have to put the needs of the club first. After today, I don't think your boyfriend is top of anyone's list. Show a little respect!''

Zara let out a sarcastic laugh. "Put the club first. Show some respect? That's rich.''

"What is your problem?'' Blake was red in the face, eyes bulging. The stress of the past few weeks hit her. She burst into tears, her hands flew to her face.

"'I'm sorry. It's the shock. I don't know why I just did that.''

The anger faded from Blake. He moved around his desk. He handed her a tissue and offered her a chair.

"Sit,'' he said, his voice was soft. "This morning has been a shock for everyone.'' Zara used the tissue to dry her eyes. ''I do care for everyone here. Jenny is a wonderful woman. I'm as angry as you are…I promise you that.''

Blake sounded sincere. "Now, take a breath and calmly tell me what this is about?''

This was a stupid move, and she had to claw her way out of it. And fast.

"If you care about the club, why would you sell it?'' she regretted her words as soon as they'd left her mouth.

The silence in the room was unsettling. Blake's eyes were wide. He slowly returned to his chair and ran his hand through his oil-black hair. It rattled him, she thought. He knew she was onto him. His reaction was unexpected. He laughed, throwing his head back.

"What?''' he was shaking his head. "Sell the club? I don't know what gossip you've been listening to.''

He stopped laughing when he saw the look on Zara's face.

"You think I am, don't you?'' he seemed genuinely bemused by her accusation.

"It's what I've heard.''

"You should know better than to listen to gossip,'' he opened his laptop, turning it to face her.

"If I were selling my club, would I be planning for the next few years?'' On the screen were plans to extend the stadium, add more shops and a few bars and a large restaurant.

"It will mean more bums in the seats and will create more jobs for the area. Would I bother if I were selling?''

"I...I...am so sorry. After the other day, and this morning, I just felt...confused, I guess. Everything just...'' Zara struggled to get her words out. It made little sense. What was going on?

"I understand you're worried about Jake, and I'm sorry you heard that. I hope Jake gets his form back.

But what I decide regarding players is none of your business. I say that in the nicest way possible.''

Alarms bells rang in Zara's head. Nothing made sense.

"It's been a stressful day. Let's forget this happened,'' Blake suggested, his smile warm and kind. He wasn't as mean and arrogant as Zara had suspected.

"I didn't mean to be so disrespectful. This won't hurt Jake, will it? I swear he has nothing to do with my outburst.''

"I thought we were forgetting it happened? And, no, I won't hold this against Jake. Despite what you might think, I want Jake to continue to be a part of this club."

Zara sighed, nodded, and stood up.

"I'll bring you some coffee, you look like you'll need it today,'' she hesitated at his door.

Debating the option of telling Blake the truth. Take the risk. They needed help. The thought was a fleeting one and she feared what result could come from that.

"Go, make sure Jenny is okay. Coffee can wait.''

Outside, players had arrived.

"Zara,'' Jake came running across the carpark. Panic on his face.

"I'm fine,'' she assured him. ''It's poor Jenny.''

Later, after giving a full statement and a medical check, Jenny was back in the kitchen, ignoring all requests to go home.

"No, I won't! My boys need feeding, and no thieving scumbag will keep me from my job,'' And that was that.

14

Jake sat across the table from Zara. The server hovered nearby.

"I can't wait for Saturday," he said a smile brightening his face as he poured more wine into Zara's glass.

Zara smiled, but it was hard for her to focus with all the new information. After Blake confirmed he was not selling the club along with the shock and confusion in his reaction, told Zara all she needed to know. He was telling the truth. She just knew it. And the hit and run involving Rosie Boxall being confirmed as a twenty-year-old out for a joy ride.

All evidence had confirmed they had arrested the right person, plus he had confessed. The robbery was still under investigation, and so far there were no clues to who had committed the crime. It could simply have been a random act. Nothing their mystery man had told them was true. Jake was calling their bluff on Saturday. They had a home game against Southampton. He was furious he'd been fooled so easily, but they had been very convincing. The fear that someone he cared about would get hurt had clouded his judgment and almost ruined his career.

"I've got a lot to repair from now on," Jake stated, determination in his tone.

Zara placed a hand over his, "You will and this all stops. Never again, will anyone make you do that, ok?" Scoring would ease the shame he felt and restore some of his integrity. "You did nothing wrong."

Jake squeezed her hand but shook his head. "I have…" he paused before continuing, his voice a whisper. "No matter how you put it, I betrayed my club, my teammates, and my friends." It was going to take a lot for Jake to forgive himself.

"That first time, I stood in the shower after, and no matter how much I scrubbed, I couldn't wash the shame away. I still haven't and I'm not sure I ever will."

"You didn't do it for personal gain. You were protecting people," deep down Zara knew, even as she said the words, many would not see it the same. "You have to forgive yourself."

"If the FA hears about this, I'm done for."

The Football Association was the governing body of Football. If you break the rules, they will get involved and investigate. Throwing matches could cause a ban from playing the sport for good. Not to mention the shame that would stick with a person for life. Jake feared both outcomes.

"Play on Saturday, like your life depends on it. The haters won't know what's hit them," Jake raised her hand to his lips and kissed it.

"Bring it on," he smiled widely. "Let's focus on the future. I'll be back to destroy any defence. I have my best mate back, and I have found the perfect woman. Things are looking up."

They toasted to the future and Zara felt happy she could enjoy fully being with Jake. Having Stevie back in his life had lifted Jake. It would take time to mend the mistakes from the past, but they were both willing to do it.

"Better lay off the wine. I want that Hat-trick," Zara reminded him.

"Consider it done," he winked. "Just the one with dinner."

He stuck to his word. He moved to water and ignoring the whispers and the sneaky picture taking from several other diners, they enjoyed their first proper date. As they paid the bill, a voice made Jake groan.

"You have got to be kidding me," Zara turned her head, and strutting towards them was Ivy Mason.

"Hello," Ivy said with a sneer. "I see you're still roughing it, Jake."

She stood behind Zara, talking over her head. She was tall, dressed from head to toe in designer clothes, dripping with diamonds. perfect hair, make-up, and tanned.

"Ivy, don't start!" Jake warned in a low tone. "Don't embarrass yourself."

She flicked her hair, and her laugh was ear-piercing.

"Me?" another laugh. "I'm not parading around with the help."

Jake banged his hand down on the table. "Don't be a bitch, Ivy. Just accept it's over and stay away from me," he turned his attention back to Zara.

"Ready?" he asked. Zara nodded. "Let's go. Don't give her what she wants."

Jake knew Ivy would have alerted the press. Winding Zara up to make her look bad was Ivy's mission. As Zara calmly put on her jacket, she faced Ivy.

"You know Ivy, I know it must embarrass you, and I know it must be hard to accept."

"What are you going on about?" Ivy snapped, eyes blazing with anger.

"Jake dumping you and dating the 'help' as you so nicely put it. Not bad for a kitchen girl," Zara smirked as Jake took her hand and walked her outside, leaving a furious Ivy behind them. He placed a kiss on her cheek as they stepped outside.

"That'll get a fair price, a picture of me kissing you."

"Jake Maddox and the Kitchen girl," Zara joked.

"A fucking hot kitchen girl," Jake replied.

Ivy followed, screaming after them. "Jake! You know she's not right for you. You're a laughingstock picking her over me. Look at her!"

Jake turned to face Ivy.

"I think you are the laughingstock. Begging a man to take you back in public? How common, Ivy. Zara is my girlfriend. Get over it. Anyway, you never wanted me. It was only about my money."

Ivy's plan for a public showdown had backfired. They left Ivy red-faced, abandoned, and alone. The Press clustered around her taking pictures. Suddenly, she no longer wanted the attention.
  "Stop taking pictures!" Ivy screamed.

15

Jake pulled on his shirt, feeling the soft material against his skin. The buzz of the dressing room felt like home. A feeling he'd hadn't felt for so long. His name lit up above his place. His heart pumped with anticipation, and he didn't need a team talk or words of encouragement. He was ready, and the clock ticked by too slowly. The pitch was where he wanted to be, with a ball at his feet. He wanted to make every fan, his teammates, manager, and most of all Zara smile today. Scoring had always been a selfish need for him, but now he wanted to do it for all those he'd betrayed.

The purple and white of the team's colours were bright against his skin. He felt the team badge on his chest under the tips of his fingers. Today he fully understood his love for his club, and the sacrifices his parents had made to get him here. They'd supported him through these past few weeks. His mother calling every day to tell him how proud she was, and he'd get through this terrible phase. His dad's words of wisdom and long talks helped guide him. How he had come so close to breaking down and telling the truth. It was Zara who changed everything. That day in the bar, and how she'd saved him without a second thought and kept his secret. She had been easy to fall for, and he could never repay her for the loyalty she had shown him. But he could try, starting today.

"You ready, Mads?" Hayden shouted across the dressing room. "Fucking need you to get your head out of your arse. Do what you've done in training this week."

His captain glared at him, and the expression was demanding. He expected results and Jake knew if he didn't deliver, Hayden would be on him with no filter. He had no excuses he could use. If he failed today, he might as well hold a sign up to say he was a lying, cheating scumbag. Hayden was suspicious already.

He crossed the room and leaned into Jake's ear, "Don't fuck this up, or I'll be your worst nightmare,"

As Hayden returned to his seat, Jake called after him, Hayden turned ready for a confrontation.

"I'm ready! I won't fail today," Jake assured him. Hayden loosened his tense stance and nodded.

"Let's get out there and show everyone we ain't fucking done!" Hayden rallied the team as the manager entered the room. "No pissing about today, we take it to them. We don't stop until they are on their knees.''

The fire in Hayden's eyes blazed as he scanned the room. His infectious personality spread like a virus. The calls from each team member reverberated around the dressing room.

"I guess I don't need to say much,'' Ted commented. ''Hayden has it covered, it seems.''

He stepped in front of the screen and reminded every player of their roles, and what he expected.

"I want to see you crawl off that pitch at the end of the game. We've let our fans down this season. People think we're a joke, and that pisses me off. You want your place on this team, you better fight for it. This is it, we lose today, and it's all but over.''

His eyes fell on Jake. "We need everyone on fire today.''

 Jake stood up. He hadn't planned on speaking, but he knew the fault lay with him.

"Lads, I know I've been shite lately. I'm sorry, but I'm ready to put that right. Get the ball to me and I'll destroy their defence today. I'm back, and I'm ready to fight.'' His words were strong and confident.

Ted approached and looked him in the eye. "Don't let me down.''

Jake nodded. Ted eyed him quizzically, before standing tall.

"You heard him, give him the ball.''

Then the bell sounded.

"Come on, let's fucking do this!'' Jake screamed, clapping his hands.

They lined up in the tunnel alongside the Southampton team. Jake focused his eyes forward, waiting for the studs of his boots to hit the pitch. When they did, he felt the striker in him awaken. The prowess of his skill he'd locked away broke free. Jake Maddox, star striker, was awake and he would show no mercy.

When the referee blew the whistle to start the game, Jake's eyes never left the ball. He tracked it like a predator. It was minutes into the game when Alvaro made a pass that sliced the Southampton midfield in half. Billy controlled the ball, turned, and ran. Jake was in a perfect position and he called for the ball. Billy flicked his eyes and pinpointed his strike partner. The pass was flawless and Jake wasted no time. He sprinted forward. Two defenders closed in, but Jake was too fast. He was a man with a mission. He could see the goalkeeper coming towards him as he left the defence behind him. The crowd screamed his name, the wall of noise powered him forward. He could see his chance. Drawing his foot back and hitting the ball with everything he had. It flew past the goalkeeper, and it nestled into the back of the net. The elation raced through him as he ran towards the fans, sliding on his knees before he was under the pile his teammates made as they bundled him to the floor.

"Yes, Mads! Fucking come on!'' Hayden screamed in his ear.

Valcoast United's fight for survival had begun. Everything had stopped inside the club as the game headed into the eighty-ninth minute. The score was 2-2.

Jake scoring both goals, his second just three minutes ago. Zara couldn't take her eyes off the match. Nothing else mattered and nobody else disagreed. There was a determination from the team that hadn't been witnessed for a long time. Every player was giving everything they had and more. The smile on Jake's face meant everything. He was in his element. He was relentless with his pressure. Once he had the ball at his feet, his speed and accuracy were destroying the Southampton defence. The fans were chanting his name, and it seemed they had forgiven him. It was beautiful to watch.

"He's back!'' Jenny said, hugging Zara. "I knew he wouldn't let us down.''

Zara could enjoy watching him play without the worry of someone getting hurt, or Jake being forced into risking his career. The atmosphere was electric. If they won this game, all they would need was to win the last game of the season and they would be safe. They would lift themselves from the relegation zone and remain in the premier league. The nightmare of this season would be over and Jake could put it all behind him.

"Yes, come on Jake!'' Jenny cried as Jake picked up a pass from Alvaro. He raced forward, the ball seemed to stick to his foot. He looked up and chipped it over the goalkeeper. Everything slowed as the ball dropped behind and bounced into the bottom right corner.

"Fucking beauty!'' Zara screamed and punched the air. She collapsed to her knees as the emotion took over. The sound of the final whistle caused her to sob. Jenny hugged her as she screamed hysterically.

"That boyfriend of yours has given me sleepless nights these past few months, but he has come back just in time.''

The sound of the crowd and those inside the club was the best thing Zara had ever heard. Pure happiness. There was hope, it wasn't over, but with Jake back in form their survival was closer than ever.

Later, as the players arrived in the players' lounge, they celebrated like it was the end of the season. Until Ted made a speech, reminding them to stay focused.

"Don't be cocky. Nothing is certain until next weekend."

It brought them back down to earth, but even Ted had a smile on his face. He clutched the whiskey in his hand like it was a lifeline. The win today had taken a little pressure off him, and the small mercy of the day's result was clear on his face. Jake smiled from across the room, watching Zara do her job. He felt nothing but pride. Crossing the room, leaning over the counter, he took her face in his hands and kissed her.

"That was the best thing ever!" he was high on life at that moment. Jake Maddox was back, but this time he was a better man. He would save his club and make sure he never let them down again.

"I'm proud of you," Zara whispered as he pulled away, and she watched him return to his teammates.

16

Zara swayed to the music. The champagne was going down a little too fast, but tonight they were letting their hair down. Jenna topped her glass off and giggled as she almost fell off the chair.

"Three points!" Jenna yelled, leaning forward using her hand to support herself. "God, I'm smashed. I haven't been out in ages. Two glasses and I'm done!" She giggled, her hand covering her mouth, then she placed a finger to her lips. "Shhh…"

Ben placed another bottle on the table, planting a kiss on his wife's cheek and winking. "Kids are with my parents. We are free tonight." It made Jenna blush and giggle again. "Keep drinking Mrs. Virgo."

"Are you trying to get me drunk?"

"Fucking right, I am," Ben said, not even hiding his excitement of having a child-free evening. "One hour and we are going."

He wasn't wasting the whole evening in the bar. That was clear. She blushed again but didn't argue. Ben left them to it.

"Is it wrong that I would like to curl up and sleep, knowing Todd won't wake me at four in the morning,'' they both laughed and opened the other bottle of wine.

"Just let him have his fun, then sleep. If it's been a while it might not take long.'' Zara suggested. "He's happy, and you get some sleep. Win, win!''

Jenna looked thoughtful.

"It's so exhausting having kids. It's not that I don't want to, I'm just shattered. But you're right, and anyway, once we get started and the champagne kicks in, he will beg me to stop.''

Jenna in her drunk state began explaining the things Ben liked.

"Oh, my god! Too much information. Stop!'' Zara begged, covering her ears. "I'm good not knowing.'' Jenna swayed as she laughed.

Jake took a seat next to Zara, his smile lighting up his face. Stevie hovered over his shoulder. The two were becoming joined at the hip, making up for lost time.

"Once that bottle is empty, we are going," he whispered in her ear, kissing her neck as he pulled away. Jenna looked knowingly at them.

"Oh, I see I'm not the only one in demand this evening," she winked and took another sip of her drink.

They had the VIP area in Vibe bar. They had roped off private space, had access to a private bar and table service, and had staff specifically for them, while the rest of the partygoers had to fend for themselves. Valcoast United players drank and danced like royalty, while onlookers observed from the other side of the rope. A face appeared in the crowd, awkwardly looking in their direction. It was Rachel, she seemed nervous as she raised her hand to wave.

"Rach!" Zara called and waved her over. She embraced her best friend over the rope. "What are you doing here?"

Rachel smiled, feeling better at the welcome.

"I was out with some girls from work, but they've gone. I saw on Instagram you were here, so I thought I'd come and say Hi."

Zara hugged her again. "You should have said you were out."

The air between them seemed off.

"You didn't tell me you were out either," an edge to her tone.

"Sorry. It's just…it was a spur of the moment thing," guilt engulfed Zara.

She hadn't been in touch as much lately. Rachel was feeling pushed out. She felt awful. "I've been a shit friend lately, I know," lifting the rope and inviting Rachel into the VIP area.

"Am I allowed?" Rachel asked, looking around as if she'd be tackled to the floor.

"Of course, you are! You're my special guest!"

This made Rachel smile, and the air warmed between them.

"Thanks!" Rachel yelled over the music as Jake handed her a glass of champagne. "It's nice to see you Jake, and this time in a better state."

Before long, she had been introduced to the rest of the group and fit in naturally.

"I'm sorry I was being a bitch…" Rachel said with guilt in her tone.

Zara stopped her.

"No. If it were the other way round, I'd have felt the same. I'm so sorry." They clinked their glasses and put it behind them. Jake put on his charm and before long Rachel was happy with her friend's latest choice of boyfriend.

They had put leaving early off. Rachel deserved more of her attention, and as they waved to Jenna and Ben as they left, Rachel pulled Zara up from her chair.

"Dance!" The music pulsed, and they let loose of the small dance floor. Jake joined them, and before long they were throwing shapes.

Alvaro and his girlfriend gyrated against each other, and a private room would have suited them better. They were a passionate couple and didn't care who saw. Beautiful and they complimented each other well.

Billy couldn't help but flirt with Rachel. Well, he tried.

"How old are you? Like twelve?" Rachel asked, and he danced away. Zara couldn't help but feel sorry for him. He looked so much younger than he was, and despite his immature ways, he meant no harm.

"That was mean!" Zara said, holding back a snigger.

"No, seriously. I was asking for real!"

"He's nineteen," Zara laughed.

"Oh shit! I didn't mean any offence. I thought he was one of the youth team," she bit her lip "Oopps".

"That's Billy Fox!"

"What! Oh bollocks!" she lifted her glass. "I've had too many of these. Did I just screw my chance of bagging a footballer?" Her sarcasm was in full force. "Well, shit."

The laughter filled the room until Zara caught something from the back of the bar. Her blood ran cold. She stopped dancing. The eyes held hers, the cap tipped forward, and shadows of dancing people flickered and shaded his face. The shake of his head, slow and deliberate, said more than any words could. A group of girls stumbled in front of her blocking her view. The room spun, but it wasn't the alcohol.

Jake grabbed her hand. He pulled her to him before anyone noticed the change in her behaviour.

"What's wrong?" his hands cupped her face. Any onlookers would assume it was just a kiss between them. She struggled to answer, but when she did, Jake turned, looking for their stalker.

"Are you sure?" he asked. Zara nodded.

"Yes. He was here. It's not over.''

He held her tightly, trying to cover the distress she was in.

"Fuck!'' he hissed. ''No. No. No.''

The celebrations were over for them. Seeing him again had snapped them back into place. ''I'll get the car to take us home.''

Rachel threw her arms around them, trying to force them back to the dance floor.

"Come on, put each other down,'' she stumbled but steadied herself quickly. Zara looked at her, her face pale.

"I'm sorry, I'm not feeling well. Jake's taking me home.'' A look of concern crossed her friend's face, followed by suspicion.

"Yeah, right? I know why you want to leave,'' she winked. The room was still spinning as panic rose in Zara's mind.

Then it went black.

17

Jake's worried voice was getting louder, like he was far away but gripping firmly, holding her as she moved.

"I think we need to call an ambulance!" Rachel said, panicking. Zara shook her head and grabbed Jake's hand. He pulled her up and wrapped one arm around her waist.

"I'm ok. I don't need an ambulance. I have just overdone it today."

The incident had caused a scene and Zara wanted to get home. It was embarrassing enough without making it worse, and with emergency services adding to the mix. This would be tomorrow's gossip. The thought made her feel sick.

"I just want to go," she whimpered into Jake's chest.

"I'll get the car," he pulled his phone from his pocket and made a call. It was short, but two minutes later they left through a private door and go into his car. When the door shut, they both let out a sigh of relief. The small mercy of privacy.

"Are you sure you're okay?" he asked, still

holding her hand.

"Yes, I've hardly eaten today and drank way too much. Seeing him just sent me into a panic.
"What happens now?'' Jake sighed heavily, the stress showing again. He'd been happy ten minutes ago, now that dark emotion was back.
"I can't do it anymore. Sunday, we have to win,'' his head was in his hands, he was so stressed. ''I can't let them down anymore.''
"So, don't,'' Zara said firmly. "Whatever happens is not your fault. Win on Sunday, we will deal with the aftermath once the season is over, and Valcoast is safe. 'We say nothing more on the matter. Sunday is your focus. Play on, Jake. No matter what, you fucking play on.''
 He stared at her. "We stick together no matter what?'' he asked, it was a question.
"No matter what,'' she promised.
They kept up the pretense once back at Jake's. He helped her out of the car. She could walk, but they knew the press would position a camera, like a sniper, waiting for them. He picked her up and cradled her, carrying her inside like a groom carrying his wife. Only this was all for show.
He kicked the door shut and gently placed her back on her feet. He imagined her in a wedding dress, a fleeting thought, but one he'd never had before. It was unnerving, but not in a way that scared him, just a new feeling. It was too soon, but he didn't rule out the possibility. He hit a button on the wall. A faint mechanical sound hummed. Security blinds descended; it now blocked all windows from any outside intrusion. He hit another button, and the

house was lit up. From the outside, it was now a fortress.

"I've never used much of the security features. But now I will."

"Why?" Zara asked.

"I have something to protect now," His eyes holding her gaze. "You."

"Oh," Zara blushed, a warm feeling coming over her and admittedly a little smugness.

"So…what now?" she asked. The alcohol held no effect anymore. The sighting had sobered her, and the fainting had killed her party mood.

"Bed," Jake quickly responded. She followed him up the stairs, pinching herself. She did that now and again to make sure she wasn't dreaming, and Jake Maddox was her boyfriend. He confirmed in his special way, he was her boyfriend. Sex with him was different, more passionate, more energetic. She could be herself, to be, or do whatever she desired. It was perfect. Even the delay while he placed protection on didn't spoil the mood. He was confident and knew exactly what he was doing. He made her lose all her insecurities.

Waking up in his bed had become her favorite place to be, warm and cozy. Only, they both had to get up and head to work. Jake made pathetic sounds beside her.

"I'm feeling like crap," he complained, rubbing his forehead. Zara laughed as she forced herself out from his grip.

"Training, Maddox! Up!"

"Spoilsport," he groaned dramatically before

dragging himself out of bed and into the shower. Zara headed to make coffee and as she passed the front door, something caught her eye. A piece of paper stuck out from the letterbox. The words written on it were:

THIS ISN'T OVER!

She wadded it up and threw it in the bin. Jake didn't need to see it. They were not being controlled anymore.

Pushing it to the back of her mind, she filled the kettle and waited for the water to boil. They had four days before the season was over. It would be the first time she had ever willed the football season to be over. Football had been a way of life in her family. It had been the thing she looked forward to. Match day with her family, no matter the weather. It was always bacon rolls for breakfast, a burger for lunch, and if they won, KFC on the way home. Thinking about her family made her heart swell. Then guilt hit her. She'd been so focused on Jake, she'd neglected them. She made her coffee and called her mum. The surprised but cheerful sound of her mother's voice made her smile.

Jake waved as he left for training. A quick call turned into an hour. Her mother still couldn't believe her daughter was dating Jake Maddox.

"It would be nice if we could meet him soon," Zara heard the hurt in her voice. "People ask me about him all the time, but I can't answer as you haven't introduced him to your parents." It was another fail on Zara's part.

"I'm sorry, mum. I promise once this season is over, I will. He's had a terrible season, and he just wants to focus on Sunday's game.''

Then her mum said something that made her stomach knot.

"Oh, I meant to tell you, we had a strange visit the other day.''

Zara stood still, nervous about what her mother would say.

"The door went and there was this man on the doorstep. It was very odd; he was looking for Jake.''

There was a pause.

"I said he didn't live here,'' her mum laughed.

"Why would someone come to our house?''

Zara was afraid to ask the next question, but she had to.

"Who was it?''

"I don't know. Never seen him before. Strange thing was, he asked if we could pass a message on? Something about… oh let me remember…I hope you've not forgotten our arrangement?''

The sound of running a tap interrupted her.

"Sorry, just filling the kettle. Anyway, I asked if he couldn't tell Jake himself. Don't you own a phone?''

Typical mum, honest and to the point.

He said he'd lost his phone. Anyway, I said I would just to get rid of him. I was in the middle of watching EastEnders and having my dinner.''

Zara sucked in her breath. It was obvious who their visitor was.

"I don't know who that would be. Anyone who

knows Jake would go to his house. I'll find out who it was.''

Her mother told her not to fuss. "It's fine. I bet it's a fan just trying his luck.''

"No, it isn't. They had no right to bother you and Dad,'' it came out more aggressive than she had intended. It alerted her mother to ask more questions.

"Wow, are you ok, Darling?'' Another sound in the background. "It's not the end of the world. I got to go, your Dad is sorting the garage out, and it sounds like he could do with some help.'' Another pause. "You can talk to me. I know there is something wrong Zara.''

"Mum don't worry. It's ok,'' Zara tried to sound convincing.

"I know when you're worried. I won't push it, but I'm here if you need to talk. Things are good with you and Jake? He's not messing you about, is he?''

Zara wanted to tell her, to have her mum tell her it would be okay, that she could make it all go away. When you're a child, parents could do that. When it's getting scary, they could chase the monsters away. Her parents couldn't chase these away, though. It was her turn to protect them. If she told her mum it would worry her, and who knows what danger it would put them in. They already knew where they lived. Plus, she didn't want them to think badly of Jake.

"We are great mum. It's just been a stressful time for him. I promise that's all.''

"Good, and we really would like to meet him.

Not because of who he is, but because he's with our daughter. We want to get to know him,'' hope in her tone.

"You'll meet him soon. I promise,'' she'd have to talk to Jake about getting them a personal tour around the grounds for next season.
Her mother seemed to accept her words and once off the phone, she tried to stay calm. The visit to her parents had thrown her peace out of the window. Zara would now spend her day off fretting over what her mother had said. The stress had crept back in after feeling free. Four days, she repeated to herself. They just had to wait another four days.

18

The days had dragged, and Jake had hardly seen Zara. He'd been training every second he could and repairing his friendship with Stevie, which had been easier than he had thought. It was as if they had never fallen out.

Zara had been amazing about it. He wouldn't be so close to getting his life back without her. He had never been in love, he knew that was certain because being with Zara was a unique feeling. She was down-to-earth, easy-going, strong, and beautiful. When he doubted himself, which he had been doing lately, she had a way of making him feel like he could do anything. A concept he'd mocked before. Others called it 'Soppy bastards' or being a 'Whipped man.'

He totally understood it. Especially for people like him. Trust was hard to find. Zara didn't seem to care about his money, and in the few months they'd been together, she asked for nothing from him. She had her own money and didn't expect to spend his too. Strangely, that made him want to spend his money on her. Maybe, just maybe, that was a clever plan.

Sunday had finally arrived, and he could feel the nerves and the excitement kicking in. Zara was already at work preparing their pre-match meals. Some might have laughed about him dating a kitchen girl, but Jake couldn't be more proud of her. His teammates thought she was a superb cook, and she was a part of the club he loved. She understood it all, loved it the same, and it helped. She would get him up, never allowing him to be late or slack off. He looked forward to ending this season and spending some quality time with her, away from the club, away from everything.

First, he had a job to do, and he planned to end the season with a performance. He felt the adrenaline pulsing through him. Parking in his usual place and jumping out of his car. His phone buzzed in his pocket, and he opened the message. His entire body froze at the picture on his screen. He used the car to steady himself, his legs couldn't hold him up and vomit rose in his throat.

"No!'' he gasped.

19

(2 hours before)

Sunday morning had arrived, finally. Zara was awake early, unable to settle during the night. Jake had spent the week training, it was all he could think about, and having Stevie back in his life had been a massive bonus. Zara had cleaned the flat, unable to sit still.

Showered and hair and make-up done, she didn't need to leave for at least another hour, but she was excited to get the day started. To pass the time, she checked up on the latest news.

The sports news was rife for the end of the season. Liverpool was set to win the premier league and Valcoast was hanging on by a thread. It was strange for Zara to read the articles. Six months ago, Jake Maddox was just a footballer, a player for the club she supported. He was now her boyfriend. The situation was still very surreal. Seeing him being talked about made her want to punch people in the face.

'He's a person, with actual feelings. He isn't an arrogant prick. You don't know him,' she raged at the television.

The vile comments made her heart hurt because she knew him. He was a caring, passionate person. A talented guy who was put under a lot of pressure. So, what if he was paid highly for it? That wasn't his fault. He didn't ask for the wages in football to be the way it was, but if those who spouted their jealous opinions had the same opportunity, they wouldn't turn it down. Zara forgot about his wealth; it wasn't something that came up often. He didn't brag about it. He went about his life and he didn't bother others. Out of her past relationships, he had been the only one who had made her feel special, loved, and confident to be herself. As she sat and thought about him, her heart swelled. If he woke up tomorrow, wasn't a footballer, and had a smaller bank account he would still be the man she wanted. She was certain of that. If their secret got out, and it all came crashing down on them, she would stand by him.

Social Media was a place Zara avoided more these days. In a moment of boredom, she braved it. Typing in Jake's name, Twitter highlighted the most recent posts. Most were football-related, under the posts were the viper pits. A few from her fainting episode, some of them in Jake's car, etc... One post was a picture of the two of them shopping in town a few days ago. Zara cringed at the sight of herself. Hair pulled back in a messy bun, bits of blonde strands escaping from it, no make-up, and dressed in jeans and one of Jake's hoodies. They looked like normal people. Jake, of course, looked perfect as usual. The comments were baffling.

Oh god, I hate her. Looks like a stuck-up cow.

He can do better than her. Can't even do her hair.

My friend's cousin went to school with her. She was snotty, bitch.

Jake, ditch the bitch.
They weren't all bad, some were nice.

I think she's pretty. Plus, she gives us normal girls hope.

I met her in Costa last week. Seemed really nice. You're all just jealous bitches.

Zara remembered being stopped in Costa. She posed for a photo. That was a strange moment. It was nice to know not everyone hated her. Again, she had done nothing to these people. How could someone judge a person they had never met? That was enough self-torture for one day. It was finally time to leave for work.
Grabbing her jacket and bag, she headed out the door. The elderly lady that lived next door was returning from walking her dog. The white poodle sniffed Zara's feet and then jumped up at her. She ruffled the dog's fur.

"Hi, Pebble," the dog barked and jumped up

again. There was some small talk with her neighbor before heading to her car.

The sun was warm already and sunbeams bounced off the car windows making her eyes squint. She pulled her keys from her bag and approached the driver's side. The silver van next to her car had parked close, so she had to turn slightly to angle the keys into the lock. There was no way she would access the car from this side.

"Fucking idiot,'' Zara cursed at the bad parking.

As she turned to walk around to the passenger side, the door of the van slid open.

It was quick. They covered her head. A powerful grip on her arm pulled her in roughly. The crack was loud as something hit the back of her head, a second of slicing pain before the darkness descended.

Then silence…

20

The picture displayed on Jake's phone burned into his mind. It silenced the sounds of the carpark. Everything slowed, bile rose in his throat. Minutes ago, he was excited, buzzing for the match. Now, he was frozen to the spot. Today he knew he could lose everything. The career he'd dreamed of since he could kick a ball was ninety minutes away from destruction.

He had a choice to make:

Save the club he loved or save the girl he loved, but he couldn't save them both.

He looked at the picture, hoping it would vanish from his phone. It didn't and his heart tore in two. Zara was bound and gagged with blood dried on her face. Her eyes were closed. The words with the picture were simple.

'Win today and she dies.'

''Oi, oi Mads, ready for it today?'' Ben's voice broke his trance.

His friend approached him, a wide smile on his face.

"You look like shit!'' he joked. As Ben got closer, his eyes narrowed, eyebrows arched in concern. "Mate, you look like you've seen a ghost.''

All banter had stopped. Ben knew something wasn't right. Jake looked at Ben, he couldn't speak, didn't know how to. His eyes screamed *'help me.'*

"Jake, what the fuck is wrong with you?'' Ben caught Jake as he collapsed to the floor, shaking and sweating. If Jake had wanted to keep his secret, fate had other ideas. Ben retrieved the phone from the floor, the picture still displayed.

"What the fuck?'' Ben hissed. "Tell me this is a joke.'' He grabbed Jake, made him look at him. "What is going on?''

"I can't drag you into this,'' Jake said.

"Fuck that!'' Ben snapped. "Where is Zara?''

Jake's response came out like a howl. "I don't know! God, they're going to kill her!''

Ben was pale, beads of sweat forming on his forehead. He read the words and looked between the message and Jake several times. It didn't take long for Ben to put the pieces together.

"Don't get involved, Ben."

"Involved in what?" he stopped and thought for a second. "No!' You…didn't! Tell me it isn't what I think!" Ben snarled, his eyes bored into Jake's.

"I had no choice."

Ben pulled Jake back to his car, "Get in and start fucking talking."
Jake didn't resist. It was a relief to tell someone, but he knew Ben had now become part of this nightmare. Once safely in the car, Jake let it all out. Once he started, he couldn't stop. Ben said nothing, his expression was murderous.
"I'm sorry. I swear to god I didn't want to do any of it. They kept telling me they'd hurt anyone I cared about. They told Zara they'd hurt Jenna and the boys. We couldn't risk it. It's sending me insane!"
Ben punched the dashboard, "Fucking scumbag!"

Jake's head hung down, "I know I am."

This was it. His career was ending. If he could get Zara back, at least he won't lose everything. Ben sucked in his breath and turned to look at his teammate.

"I'm not talking about you. Some wanker I don't know threatened my family? You put your career on the line to protect them?" he questioned.

Jake couldn't look at Ben, too ashamed. "I'm sorry.''

Ben patted Jake on the shoulder, "You were protecting my family. I'd do the same if it was me. I hate that you've betrayed the team, but you had no choice.''

"What do I do now?'' Jake asked. Ben didn't answer at first. He was thinking…his focused face.

"There is only one thing to do,'' he called his wife. "Jenna, listen to me. Get the boys and head to the club, now.'' Jake couldn't make out Jenna's response. "I can't explain now. Just trust me, get to the club with the boys. Make sure you turn on any tracking device, even the secret ones.''

Another pause as Jenna demanded to know what Ben was talking about.

"Damn it, women, do it. I'll explain after the game. Stay visible to any cameras, press, etc. Stay visible!'' Jenna stopped protesting. Her husband's voice told her he wasn't joking.

"Ok.'' Jake heard her say.

"I guess we both have a job to do," Ben was calm.

"No! Fuck that. You are not doing it," Jake argued. "No way!"

"I can. You have protected my family," he paused. "Now, I need to help you protect yours."

Jake's head was in his hands, "You can't."

"You love her, don't you?" Ben stated.

"Yes, I do and I know what I have to do on that pitch. You don't have to compromise yourself," Jake said with force.

Ben rubbed his forehead. He let out a long sigh, "Yes, I do. Jenna thinks the world of Zara and she hasn't had anyone she could trust in a long time. She'd never forgive me if I allowed something to happen to her. Plus, she's part of this club. We are family, right?"

"I wouldn't have done it if I didn't give a shit, but he threatened Jenna, James, and Todd. There was no way I was risking it," Jake went on.

"When we find the prick, I'll kill him myself," Ben snarled. "Next season we will make it right. Let's just get Zara safe."

Ben had decided and Jake felt instant relief knowing

that he had an ally on the pitch. Jake hated the sacrifice Ben was making, but they both had no choice.

"Thanks, mate. I will owe you for life,'' Jake promised.

"Yeah, fucking too right. I will rinse you for this,'' Ben said, joking with an underline of truth. They composed themselves before heading inside pretending to be ready to win.

21

The pain at the back of Zara's head pounded, and any movement hurt. Her sight was black, the blindfold tied tightly. They had bound her hands and feet together. The ties were cutting into her skin. A gag muffled her cries. The smell of cigarettes and dampness hung in the air. She could hear a faint sound in the distance, in another room she guessed.

"Fuck you!'' a male voice yelled. "Payback is a fucking bitch.'' They cackled at something.

Zara lay still and tried to focus on the sound.

What was it? A familiar voice filtered through, but she couldn't put her finger on it. Then the male voice screamed in delight.

"Yes, fucking get in!''

The sound of a crowd cheering. The penny dropped. It was a football match. Valcoast United, she betted.

Did Jake know? Was he playing?

She cried out. Despite the gag, she made enough noise to alert her abductor. Footsteps approached, and a gulping sound as if they were drinking. They were close, she could hear their breathing.

''You're awake. I'm watching the game,'' the tone of his voice was calm, friendly as if they were friends. "City just scored.''

Laughter followed.

"Not the best start. Good for me though.''

She felt a tug on the gag and they pulled it down to her chin.

"Help me!'' She screamed. "Please.''

"I wouldn't bother. Nobody can hear you.''

Strong hands grabbed her arms and lifted her to her feet.

"Come with me. You won't want to miss this.''

He dragged her roughly before being placed upright

on something more comfortable. The sound of the game was louder now. The commentator's excited voice making the calls.

"It's Maddox, down the middle. Oh no, how did he miss that?" the crowd roared with anger.

They pulled the blindfold from her eyes. A TV was the first thing she saw and a replay of Jake's miss. The shot of the fans angrily hurling abuse at him. Her heart broke.

"He knows I'm here, doesn't he?"

There was no attempt to look at her captor. All her attention was on the screen. There was a movement to the side of her. She turned to look at him, knowing it would be Cap man.

He came into vision, and her mouth dropped open.

"Hello Zara," he said, the fake accent dropped.

"You!" Zara hissed. The face she saw was unexpected. "Why?"

An evil grin on his face.

"It's time for payback."

22

The anger from the crowd was growing. There were no excuses he could give. The look on his manager's face was fury. He had to stay on the pitch, but he would be substituted soon. Today was too important. He thought about Zara, her words from the other day:

'Whatever happens, you play on.'

But he couldn't. Hayden screamed at him. "Jake, what is your fucking problem. Wake up.''

All eyes were on him as he took the corner. It curled into the box, Alvaro jumped and nodded the ball into the back of the net. They were level.

"Better,'' Hayden yelled as he pointed at him. "Now, get your head back in the game.''

The equalizer would give him a chance of staying on. The pressure was getting to him. Hatred and anger towards him would get worse. No longer the fan-favorite that was slowly dying. He could hear the crowd, and they were not singing his name. He wanted to scream at them all. Tell everyone, if he didn't do this, his girlfriend would die. That Ben was only doing this to save her. Ben shouldn't have to do this. He was putting his career at risk. The responsibility of all of this was soul-destroying. The thought made him choke.

Manchester City made a run towards the goal. Jamie Boxall tracking the striker and intercepted. He turned and booted it down the middle, it was intercepted by the City midfield. Jake watched the ball and made a run up the pitch. It happened fast, a powerful kick that hurled the ball over the Valcoast defenders. Ben dived to save it. He connected with the ball. It flicked over his hand and it was in. The score now 1-2 to Manchester City.

Jake knew Ben could have saved that. His friend's head was down. The feeling Jake felt that first time was now taking hold of the goalkeeper. It was devastating. No one would ever find out. Even if Jake came clean, he would never throw Ben to the wolves. As half-time approached, Jake welcomed the chance to breathe and think. It was nearly over.

23

Zara stared in disbelief. No, she hadn't woken up. It was a dream.

"I don't understand,'' her mind was in chaos, and it made no sense. This couldn't be real.

"I know…it's a shock, but don't worry, you won't suffer. It's just time Jake had it all taken away. Like I did,'' he sighed.

"You can't trust anyone these days,'' he sniggered. "Don't worry, you won't miss the second half. I want you to watch your precious Valcoast United humiliated at the hands of Jake.''

Another laugh, this time more sinister.

"Then when he has betrayed everyone. I will make him watch as I kill you. Then I'll make sure everyone knows he's a cheat.''

"Stevie,'' Zara choked out. "He's your friend. Why?''

"Friend!'' Stevie snapped. "He's no friend of mine. He always got what he wanted. I got nothing. I worked hard, but it didn't matter. It was never me. Jake Maddox was all anyone cared about.'' Stevie spoke with loathing.

The friendly guy she'd spent getting to know didn't exist. There was nothing in his eyes, just darkness.

"Jake thinks the world of you. He's so happy to have you back in his life," Zara said, as calmly as possible. Stevie pulled a repulsed look. "He's   a selfish, arrogant prick!" Stevie took another swig of the vodka bottle. "He got the looks, career, and any girl he wanted."

His fists balled, "Me? I was just the mate that tagged along, always overlooked, and when I finally got a break, a chance to show my talent. It was taken away."

His head went down and his hands grabbed it. His legs shook, and he ranted.

"Why was I not good enough?" he screamed in her face. She reeled back in fear. "Then I saw you. I wanted you but no, Jake won, again."

"What are you talking about? I was already with Jake when we meet."

Stevie snorted, "I saw you first."

"What?"

"I was at the club the day you started," he said. "No, we didn't meet, but I was there in the restaurant at one point. Of course, you didn't notice me, but you noticed him. Everybody notices Jake Maddox. Nobody gives a shit about Stevie Howe."

He kicked out at the table in front of them, tipping it over. Lighting a cigarette with his shaking hands as he stood.

"Have you any idea how it feels to be the pathetic friend?" he reached for a Tesco bag on another chair and pulled out another large bottle of Vodka. He drank from the bottle and he seemed to calm after that.

"This has been my only friend. I tried to stop, but I decided I don't want to,'' he tapped the side of his head. ''Stops the chaos in my mind.''

"Stevie, please. Don't do this.''

"Shut the fuck up. You have no idea what a piece of shit he is. I want to see him suffer!'' he screamed, spittle splashing her face. "He...he doesn't give a shit about me.''

"What did he actually do? He was better than you at football. He's better looking, and he didn't get injured and lose the chance to play? That's your reason for all this?'' Zara screamed, fear and desperation gripping her.

"Yes.'' Stevie replied, ''and I can't forgive him.''

"You can't forgive him for what? Because life dealt you a different hand. Everything he has was never yours.''

"He slept with my girlfriend!'' Stevie yelled. "I thought, for the first time I had got the girl, bet you didn't know that part,'' he thought he'd revealed a shocking secret.

"I know and that was wrong. He regrets it. That was the only thing he did, everything else wasn't his fault,'' Zara pleaded.

Stevie flung out his arm, hitting her across the face. "Stop talking,'' he leaned over her. "It's always the same. He just wins all the time.''

"He's not winning now!'' Zara snapped back. "You wanted to take away his career? Well done, you've done it. Now, let me go!''

Stevie shook his head. "No, I want him to lose everything he cares about. I never thought I'd hear

Jake talk about being in love. He told me all about you. He couldn't shut up. Zara this, Zara that. How amazing you are, blah, blah. He was never the committed type. I hadn't planned on hurting you but killing you would break him.''

The sound of the TV interrupted them. The second half was seconds away.

"Turn it off!'' Zara screamed.

"No. Watch it,'' he pulled her back up to a sitting position. His hold on her was tight. "You can't stop them going down, or Jake losing his halo and you won't be alive to comfort him. He will be alone. Just like I was!''

Tears stung as they escaped and ran down her cheeks. "This is unfair. None of this was his fault. He's your friend, please! You're hurting the whole club.''

"Shut up!''

"No. If the club goes down, it won't just be Jake who suffers. What if people lose their jobs because of it? What did they do wrong? The rest of the team did nothing, you're making them suffer too.''

"Don't be dramatic. That club has plenty of money.'' Stevie's foot caught on a pile of plastic bags as he stepped backward. They used the bags in the club shop. Several fell on their sides. Bundles of money spilled out onto the floor. Zara gasped, and she gaped at the wave of money flowing from the bags.

"It was you!'' Zara accused. "You robbed the club and attacked Jenny.''

"I didn't hurt her,'' Stevie justified it. "Plus, they owed me.'' There was no remorse.

"Nobody owes you anything. Jenny didn't deserve that, she did nothing wrong.''

There was no point in her rant, he didn't care, but she said it, anyway.

"Look, she's fine. I needed money. They offered me an insulting amount of money to train those... unworthy..."

"No, you just couldn't stand to see others have what you lost. You're pathetic."

Stevie seethed, eventually leaving her alone for a few minutes. When he returned, Zara noticed the glint of metal from the corner of her eye. The large kitchen knife swung by his side. He was teasing her with it. Her heart pounded, and her mouth was dry, fear running through every nerve. He saw it on her face, and he smiled. He was enjoying the game he had created.

"I was going to be kind," he mused, pressing the knife against her cheek. "I was going to make it quick..."

A loud, rapid knocking stopped him from completing his sentence.

"Fuck sake."

"Steve, let me in. Stop!" Zara recognized the voice straight away. Cap man. Stevie looked irritated before leaving her to let him in.

"You lied!" Cap man shouted. Panic mixed with anger, but mainly fear. Footsteps approached the door to the shabby living room they held her captive in. He wore no cap or any face covering. He was younger than she'd assumed. Maybe, twenty. Greasy brown hair pulled back in a man bun, a skull tattooed on his neck. The menacing look he'd used on previous meetings no longer on his face.

"Has he hurt you?" he asked. His voice was kind and

relieved to see her.

"Like you care!" Zara snapped. His eyes couldn't meet hers, guilt radiated from him.

"Chill out Tommy boy. She's fine, for now.''

Strangely, knowing cap man's name made him more human, less sinister. Tommy turned to face Stevie.

"You said nothing about murder! I didn't sign up for this. Just mess with them, you said and I'm still waiting for my money. So, pay up and I'll disappear."

Stevie put his hand in his pocket. "You're right, it's only fair.''

There was a smirk on his face. He pulled a five-pound note out of his pocket.

"Here. Buy yourself something nice,'' he flicked it and it landed by Tommy's feet.

"You fucking prick. You said ten grand. I need that money!"

Stevie snorted, "I'm sorry to disappoint, but I don't have that kind of money. That fiver I offered is the best I can do.''

Zara didn't stop to consider her next move. "How about the money you robbed from the Club?'' Tommy spun to look at her, "What?!''

Zara tilted her head toward the spilled money, Tommy hadn't noticed on his arrival. The outrage came out like a firebolt.

"I'll kill you!'' Tommy screamed. "You said that had nothing to do with us, it was just a random event, like the kid.''

Tommy paused, "Wait, that was random, right?''

Stevie chuckled, "Don't get sentimental now, Tom.

You were fine about this when you thought there was ten grand on the table...''

Stevie sucked in a deep breath, "That little brat was just unlucky, it had nothing to do with us. However, it gave me more to punish Jake with. Watching him suffer from the guilt was satisfying. I wish I had done it.''

"You're sick!'' Tommy yelled, balling his fists. "I know I helped you, a decision I regret now. Let her go, it's over. You hurt her and I'll blow this shit wide open. I'll take my punishment but I won't let you murder an innocent girl.''

Zara could see his loyalty switching, Tommy looked back at her, "I didn't want this... I swear.''

"How sweet,'' Stevie mocked. "She's spoken for, kid. Likes the rich players, not little people.''

Tommy swung his fist and knocked Stevie to the floor.

"Fuck you!'' he screamed over and over as he kicked him repeatedly until Stevie lay still, and Zara stared in disbelief at his lifeless body.

"I won't hurt you,'' Tommy said calmly. "I know you have every right to doubt me. You can trust me, I'll get you out of here. I promise.'' He slowly approached, hands out, "I won't hurt you. I never intended to.''

"I need to get to the game, to Jake.''

"I'll take you there,'' he assured her.

"I need him to know I'm ok.''

The Television was still on, the score was now a draw at 2-2 and there was only thirty-five minutes left.

"I need to go now!'' Zara screamed.

Tommy couldn't release her tied hands and feet with bare hands.

"I'll get a knife."

"Stevie had one!" Zara cried. "Hurry up!"

It was still in his hand. He was so shocked at Tommy turning on him, he'd had no chance to use it.

"I'll get you out!" Tommy turned and bent to retrieve the knife.

When he cut her free, she sprung from the sofa. There was no time to wait. Heading to the door, she could feel the adrenaline pulsing through her. Then she heard a thud. She stopped and turned.

"No!" Zara screamed as Tommy fell to the floor, a knife in his back. Stevie stood over him.

"One down," Stevie said with a snigger as he pulled the knife out of Tommy's back. "You're next."

To the side of Zara were several piles of wood, her only weapon. She grabbed one just in time before he jabbed the knife in her direction. The wood shielded her, but it wouldn't hold for long. The force caused Stevie to lurch backward. He winced as his knee twisted. His injured knee and she remembered what Jake had said:

'His injury was severe. Damaged his left knee. It healed enough so he could walk, but not to play football. Specialist doctors said it was too weak.'

Zara had one chance to escape, and this was it.

"Zara, you can't outrun me. I can still run and I'm pretty fast," he bragged.

"Really," she said, a cold expression on her face.

"Try me," he threw back.

"Left is it, Stevie?" she hissed with venom. She gripped the wood and swung, slamming it against his left knee. The howl he let out was ear-shattering.

"Catch me now, Stevie! This is over just like your career!"

She swung it down again on his other knee. The snap of bones made her feel sick. He let go of the knife to hold his knees.

"You fucking bitch. I'll kill you."

"I doubt it," Zara laughed, making a lunge for the knife. "Move and I'll bury this in your skull. I have a game to get to and a club to save."

"No!" Stevie yelled as he grabbed her ankle. "I'll ruin Jake, and that fucking club. And all the little people in it."

He pulled her leg, causing her to lose her balance. He gripped both ankles and crawled up the length of her body. His hand reached for the knife, and they wrestled with each other.

"You won't get out of this house, not alive anyway," he overpowered her, snatching the knife away. He held it against her throat, the sharp steel cut into her skin.

"I wanted him to watch," Stevie gritted out.

Just as Zara sobbed knowing death was inevitable, Tommy appeared above them, bloodied but alive. He pulled the crazed Stevie from her.

"Stop, Steve," Tommy said trying to grab the knife. It became a battle between the two of them. Fists flew at each other, blood-splattered as they rained blows down on each other.

"Go Zara, Run!" Tommy screamed. He was on the floor, losing blood rapidly as Stevie towered over him.

"Go!" Tommy wouldn't survive the fight, his wound

too deep. Something in Zara snapped. Could she walk away and leave Tommy to his death? He'd protected her. Saved her? If she ran, Stevie would take everything away from Jake. He'd destroy the club she'd love and supported all her life. If she escaped, they would never be free. Stevie was too far gone in his vendetta. His hatred for Jake was deep-rooted, misguided, and she knew he would never stop.

All her emotions shut down, apart from her love for Jake and Valcoast United football club.

The knife lay to the side of the battling men. She grabbed it as Stevie lifted his fist to give the final blow to Tommy. He noticed her coming for him.

"No!" Stevie screamed as she buried the knife in the side of his neck. He gripped the wound as the blood spurted out. He fell backward and writhed on the floor.

"You were right about one thing. Jake and I are a team. One you underestimated. This is your final whistle, Stevie Howe," she whispered as he took his last gurgled breath, then she collapsed in shock.

Blood oozed from Stevie, and his eyes went vacant. Tommy groaned as he sat up,

"Zara, you need to go."

There was no time to go to pieces. She had to get to Jake, nothing else mattered.

"What about you?" she asked,

"You owe me nothing. I was a fool, owed so many people money. He pulled me into this after drinking in a pub. It went too far. I'll handle this mess. You were never here. Take my car."

Wasting no time, she grabbed her bag and looked at

herself in the bathroom mirror. Blood splatters covered her face and jumper. She grabbed a tatty-looking towel from the dirty floor and scrubbed the blood away. Stevie lived out of town, on a farm a short drive from The Arch stadium.

Tommy threw her his keys. "I'm sorry," he said as she caught them.

"I think we're even Tommy" A few seconds passed as they locked eyes. "Thank you."

"Go, Zara. Now!"

Adrenaline pulsed through her, and the getaway car was waiting. The key ignited the engine, and it roared to life.

She raced from the uneven, weed-stricken drive of the farm. The house grew distant in the mirror. Sobs escaped her. She was a murderer. Would Jake hate her for killing his best friend? It was self-defense, she told herself. Wasn't it?

24

As Zara got closer to the Stadium, heart pounding, the commentary on the radio was overwhelming. The score was still the same with ten minutes left. Zara abandoned the car two streets away and ran. She prayed for injury time, this time they needed it. Her muscles ached from the sprint, stopping for nothing. The streets were quiet. Most people were inside the ground. Then the gate appeared, and she flew through it, her pass letting her through smoothly. It was just a minute to the player entrance, her quickest way in.

"Zara, where have you been?" one of the security men said as she approached. "Damn girl, slow down." He chuckled grabbing her.

"Please let me in this way! I need to get in there. Jake won't be happy I missed the game. I need to get inside quickly."

He thought before smiling, "If you can make him bloody score and win this game."

Zara nodded, "He will."

"Fine. Hurry. I didn't see you." Zara blew him a kiss as she sprinted inside.

Taking every step with precision until the changing rooms were in her sight, running up the stairs and along the tunnel.

"Zara!" the voice made her stop, she turned to face her boss. "Where the hell have you been?"
Jenny's expression changed, and annoyance turned to concerned.

"What's happened? You look like shit, no offence."

Zara looked between her boss and the tunnel exit.

"None taken. I'll explain, I promise. I can't now."
Zara sprinted toward the exit.

"Zara!"

The roar of the crowd powered her forward. The atmosphere hit her as she emerged from the tunnel. Ted facing the pitch, his back to her, shrieking instructions to his players. Four minutes left and still a draw. Her eyes scanned the pitch, searching for Jake. Then she saw him. She had to get his attention without causing too much focus on her. Staying just on the fringes of the tunnel, she waited for a moment to catch his eye. Time was running out, she'd gone through too much to fail now.

"JAKE!" her scream traveled. All the players on the benches turned to look. Ted did a double-take.

"Zara? You can't be here."

"Ted. He needs to know I'm here."

"What?" a confused look on his face. "I don't have time for this." He turned away.

Zara took a few steps towards him.

"Ted, if you want to win this game. Jake needs to know I'm here."

There were a few seconds of silence between them.

He seemed to understand, an unspoken conversation that he had to do as she said but he didn't need to know why.

"Are you alright, girl?'' he asked, his voice low.

"I will be once Jake sees me, and so will he.'' Ted's face gave nothing away, he checked his watch. He turned back to the game and shouted.

"Maddox, focus lad!'' Jake didn't respond until Ted's voice boomed his name. "Fucking get your head out ya arse Jake, or I'll drop you next season.'' Jake heard that and looked over at the technical area. He did a double-take as he took in his girlfriend's face.

"Play on,'' she silently mouthed.

It was as if someone had flicked a button on. Jake called upfield to Ben, nodding towards Zara. Ben followed his gaze and looked back at Jake, his eyes wide. A nod of the head told the goalkeeper his part in this was over. He took control of his goal, a sentry for his club. The look in his eyes meant nothing was getting past him.

Jake called for the ball, his demeanor changed, and he morphed into the player he truly was. The ball passed smoothly between the midfield. Jake made the run. He was in perfect space. Hayden made a vigorous pass, easy for Jake to collect. Everything hung on these last few seconds.

"Come on!'' Zara screamed. "Don't lose that fucking ball. The defense was on him, but he eluded them.

"Get forward, all of you!'' Ted yelled.

The match official held up the board to show injury time.

Three minutes.

That was all the time they had left. One goal was all they needed to stay in the premier league. The chanting and desperate shouts vibrated around the ground. The passionate desire to win, the anticipation, dread, excitement, and hope all rolled into one. Jake threatened the Manchester City goal, each attempt getting closer to a goal. His poor form fell from him as he shook off any doubt. Jake Maddox wasn't done, he was just getting started. Billy went up for a header, knocking it down into Jake's path. Now was Jake's chance. All he had to do was keep his nerve and focus and not mess this up.

He was in the penalty box, and as he prepared to fire the ball at the goal. A crunching tackle took him down.

''No! Ref!'' Ted shouted, waving his arms in the air like he was possessed. The players surrounded the referee. Zara cried out in frustration. If they disallowed the penalty, it was all over. ''It was a penalty!'' Every voice called out.

The wait was gut-wrenching as the referee debated with the linesman. Then, when all hope seemed lost, he pointed to the penalty spot. Jake grabbed the ball. There was no way he wouldn't take that chance.

Zara watched and timed slowed. This was the last kick of the game. Several match officials had tried to move her, but her fierce screams made them back off.

"Come on, Jake! Please,'' she whispered to herself. Her hands only half-covering her eyes, Jake placed the ball on the spot. He took a few steps back, took a few seconds to visualize it, and then he moved. His leg went back and as his boot hit the ball the sound it made was unmistakable. It was powerful, precise, and unstoppable.

The ball flew as if it had been shot from a cannon. The net rippled and then the roar from every Valcoast United player, management and fan was like a tidal wave crashing over them. They called for the final whistle, every voice shrieking with desperation. Then the referee blew his whistle and The Arch Stadium erupted.

"He did it!" Ted yelled as he threw his arms around her. "He's only fucking done it."

Ted planted a kiss on her forehead. He looked down at her. "I have no idea what all that was about, but after that, I don't care," he winked and released her to run on the pitch.

Zara laughed as chaos descended.

Fans invaded the pitch, and the chaos was nothing but elation.

Through the crowd, a shell-shocked Jake emerged, his eyes scanned around until they landed on Zara. He ran to her and picked her up, kissing her.

"Zara! Are you okay?" his first thought was her. She held onto him, sobbed into his neck.

"I am now. It's over, Jake. It's finally over. You did it!"

"You did it!" he kissed her again. "What happened?" he asked.

Zara pressed her forehead against his.

"I'll tell you everything, but not here. Let's just enjoy this moment."

He wiped her tears away. "It doesn't matter what you did," he assured her.

"Even if I had to do something terrible?" Jake saw the trauma in her eyes.

"Whatever you did, you did to survive, right?"
he saw her fear, the distress as she nodded.
"To protect you. I... I love you, Jake. I couldn't let
him take all this away." her eyes took in the scene,
the smile on Jake's face.
He'd done what he didn't think was possible. He
was where he was born to be, on a pitch with a ball
at his feet. He stroked her cheek, pulled her to him,
and kissed her.
"I love you too," he whispered. "I've got it from
here. It's my turn to protect you."

Delirious fans surrounded them. To anyone looking
on, Jake Maddox was celebrating the club's survival
and his return to form. What nobody would ever
know was just what that kitchen girl had gone
through to protect Valcoast United, Jake, and
herself.

Epilogue

Zara watched as the news reporter gave the update. A tear ran down her cheek. A tear for her sorrow, guilt but ultimately anger that Stevie had given her no choice.

''Stevie Howe's funeral takes place at 3pm today. The tragic life of the promising footballer has been revealed. Reports say he never handled the loss of his career. He was an alcoholic and had racked up over sixty thousand pounds of gambling debt. Evidence also revealed he was behind the robbery at Valcoast United a few weeks ago. Tommy Bassett pleaded guilty to the murder of Stevie Howe. The two were working together and after a dispute over money, promised to Mr. Bassett after the robbery, he stabbed him in the neck. He awaits trial in the coming weeks.''

Jake turned the Television off.

''He kept his word.'' Zara said, grateful to the man she used to fear.

''He owed you that.'' Jake took her hand. ''It's time to move on, you did nothing wrong. I made you a promise. I intend to keep it. There is no way they can connect you to any of it. I've made sure of it.

Only Ben, Jenna, Ted, and Jenny know the truth, and all of us have a lot to lose. I have ensured you're safe." His tone was firm and final. After the game they couldn't hide the truth, they had understood. Horrified by it. Ted wanted to keep his prized player, and avoid any punishment the club would endure, and Jenny was still suffering from PTSD because of the attack. Jenna Virgo would have killed him herself after threatening her babies and for what Ben had to do, to save Zara. "We can trust them." His kissed her cheek. "You are safe. I've got you, always." Jake held onto her, another kiss on the top of her head. He had his career back, and he looked forward to a new future with the women he planned to marry.

"Now, start unpacking." He handed her a key, a key to her new home. A new start and a new season waited for them.

ABOUT THE AUTHOR

Deep in the heart of Portsmouth, England, lives a quirky Brit with a larger-than-life imagination.

Meet Kat Green!

Music and the Military have been major influences in Kat's life and has shaped the woman she is today. Kat moved around frequently growing up which afforded her the opportunity to meet new people and experience many different bands broadening her music library.

Writing was always an afterthought, but when she lost her Mum to cancer in 2010, it was time to put words to paper. Life is too short.

Kat's books span the rock star romance genre adding a hint of mystery with her Black Eagles Series. Or if you need a paranormal thriller to keep you looking over your shoulder at night, check out Veiled, Frozen Pact, or her latest release, Listen To Me! Either way, you will not be disappointed.

Please feel free to follow Kat on various social media platforms so you never miss out on a new release!

Facebook: https://www.facebook.com/KatGrn00/
Amazon: https://www.amazon.com/Kat-Green/e/B00L2MQE0A
BookBub: http://bit.ly/2Wiu4g9
Twitter: https://twitter.com/Katwrites00

KAT GREEN

Printed in Great Britain
by Amazon

82044887R00130